Potomac Review

Potomac Review

EDITOR
John Wei Han Wang

POETRY EDITOR
Katherine Smith

NONFICTION EDITOR
Albert Kapikian

COVER DESIGN & ILLUSTRATIONS
Ash Weaver

ADMINISTRATIVE ASSISTANT
Om B. Rusten

ASSOCIATE EDITORS

Dianne Bosser

Courtney Ford

Robert Giron

Mariko Hewer

Michael Landweber

Michael LeBlanc

Kateema Lee

David Lott

Mike Maggio

Yeve Montgomery

David Saitzeff

Jessie Seigel

Marianne Szlyk

Karolina Wilk

INTERNS

Amiela Arcellana

Caleb Berer

Isabella Bergman

Mikaela Columba

Mary-Kate Wilson

Nicholas Tracy

Potomac Review is a journal of fiction, poetry, and nonfiction
published by the Paul Peck Humanities Institute at
Montgomery College, Rockville
51 Mannakee Street, Rockville, MD 20850

Potomac Review has been made possible through
the generosity of Montgomery College.

A special thanks to Dean Elizabeth Benton.

For submission guidelines and more information:
www.potomacreview.org

Potomac Review, Inc. is a not-for-profit 501 c(3) corp.
Member, Council of Literary Magazines & Presses
Indexed by the American Humanities Index
ISBN: 978-0-9990403-8-6
ISSN: 1073-1989

SUBSCRIBE TO POTOMAC REVIEW
One year at $24 (2 issues)
Two years at $36 (4 issues)
Sample copy order, $12 (single issue)

TABLE OF CONTENTS

FICTION

Hyan Hyun-Ock Im
A RELAXING DAY 1

Jennifer Savran Kelly
THE ELEVATOR 28

Banzelman Guret
A NEW REVENUE STREAM 70

Christopher Heffernan
GRANNY 86

Len Kruger
DOCKLESS 100

Christian Holt
A GRAVE FOR EVERY SHITTY MAN 114

Mary Lynn Reed
ONCE IN FLORENCE, ALABAMA 156

POETRY

Francine Witte
HOW THE LIGHT HITS 25

Rooja Mohassessy
STRANIERA 26

Patricia Budd
ABSENT EVERYWHERE 39

TWILL TIES 40

Naomi Thiers
THE GIRL WHO COULDN'T SEE HER TURQUOISE 42

Bill Christophersen
THANKSGIVING DAY 65

Deborah Allbritain

FROM THE KITCHEN IN MARCH 66

DAY AFTER VALENTINE'S 68

. MY DAUGHTER TEXTS A PICTURE AND

CALLS IT REHAB BRAIDS 69

Maegan Gonzales

THE OTHER SIDE OF THE WOMB 83

I AM THINKING OF FEEDING MY EARS TO MY FAMILY 84

Jason Gebhardt

GRAPES 89

Gary Fincke

PENTECOSTAL 90

Benjamin Balthaser

DISMANTLING 97

Eddie Krzeminski

JIMMY JOHN'S 98

Peter Serchuk

THE RECORD 113

Ed Falco

X ON FEAR & JOY 132

X AND THE SPIDER 134

Maryann Corbett

CONTAINMENT 154

AFTER THE GREAT SICKNESS, WE GO OUT AGAIN 155

NONFICTION

Chris Vanjonack

YOU WILL UNDERSTAND AFTER ENTERING 44

Amanda Gaines

PURPLEST 92

Rita Welty Bourke

THE FAR-FLUNG DAUGHTERS OF MOTHER SETON 136

CONTRIBUTOR BIOS 174

Ritchie handed the noodles back to him, with the
hint of a smile. "You might even enjoy yourself."

A RELAXING DAY

Michel, now just another piano player at a dive where men of means went slumming with their young tarts, looked through the picture window into a night laden with futility. Le fin. The credits rolled. Jeffrey Brown made a mental note to ponder the absurdity of existence on the bus ride home.

When the lights came on, Jeffrey saw a slightly built man in a leather jacket who'd slept through the film. He was a diagonal line, across the profile of the chair, secured by the resistance of his shoes against the floor. A young woman in a petal pink beret shook his shoulder to wake him up.

The cineastes exited the screening room, but curiosity compelled Jeffrey to stay behind to take a closer look at the sleeping man. He had time: he was fifteen minutes ahead of schedule. He'd spent weeks creating a schedule of relaxing activities, with the objective of achieving maximum relaxation before the next day's momentous event. He would compete with Mormon missionary Brigham "Brig" Larsen for the Korean Language Achievement Award on Korea's most popular variety show, *March of Happiness*.

The manager rounded up the folding chairs, stacking them in the back of the room where the projectionist was unspooling the last reel of the film. The clamor of chairs roused the sleeping man, who lifted his head with a bemused smile as if emerging from a pleasant dream. His long hair fell back into place, revealing an enigmatic face of finely drawn features. Jeffrey placed his hand over his heart. Was this a beauty that provoked agony in the eye of the beholder? He had no time to answer because Beret Girl was looking at him; she thought he was looking at her. He averted his

1

eyes, blinking rapidly, and pretended to look for something in his bag. Embarrassment was the bane of his existence. Life was replete with unforeseen circumstances. What was he looking for again? He pulled out his journal and wrote about the *film français* he'd just seen.

The couple got up to leave. Jeffrey fumbled with his bag as he followed them down a steep flight of stairs. They were headed in the same direction. Beret Girl gripped Sleeping Man's arm to keep herself from slipping on a sidewalk coursed with rivulets of ice. His hair was tucked under his jacket to conceal its length. A week after his arrival in Seoul, Jeffrey had seen a policeman chase a long-haired youth for several blocks, and once caught, the policeman had sheared off the youth's hair with a hefty pair of scissors. Long hair was a violation of the Minor Offenses Act, as were short skirts and kissing in public. Jeffrey had the long list of offenses stored in his head. It was 1982. Just three years ago, there had been a military coup d'état.

There was a high demand for English teachers in a country immersed in the throes of industrialization, waving its sooty hand to the First World. While Jeffrey was eminently qualified, most Westerners got teaching positions simply by being native speakers of English. The truth was, Jeffrey wasn't very interested in Korea; he was interested in French culture and Japanese culture. He'd wanted to study *ikebana* in Japan, but that was impossible without living expenses. Working in Korea would enable him to make trips to Japan.

It was the coldest day of the year, yet the couple weren't wearing proper winter coats, which many Koreans didn't seem to have, dashing from building to building for respite from the frigid peninsular winters. Jeffrey's coat was adequate, but he despaired that the subzero hunting parka he'd ordered from Eddie Bauer hadn't arrived yet.

The couple joined the crowd at the No. 38 bus stop. Jeffrey's stop was a few blocks away, but he stopped to take a mental snapshot of a face he didn't want to forget just as the bus arrived, swerving to a stop on a slick of black ice. Sleeping Man melted into the throng rushing to board the bus. Jeffrey edged closer to catch a glimpse of him and was swept upward, into the bus, by a current of people pushing and shoving to get on.

When the bus began to exceed carrying capacity, the driver pulled the handle, slamming the door shut — before Jeffrey could get off. He gunned the accelerator, throwing Jeffrey onto the lap of a schoolgirl who he saw cry out in pain. Mortified, he jumped off her and fell to the floor; she moved over to the window seat — just behind Sleeping Man — to let him take a seat.

The bus moved at roughshod speed but not fast enough for Jeffrey. This bus mishap was throwing him off schedule. He calculated the schedule of relaxing activities would stay on course if he got off at the next stop and run to the No. 47 that would take him home — where he could resume relaxation. Meanwhile, he'd gaze at the man seated by the window, nodding here and there to what Beret Girl said. He wondered how long the two had been together.

His thoughts turned to the competition. It had two components: Cultural Assimilation Performance and Conversation Proficiency. Brig, his rival, would sing a medley of chart-topping pop songs. Not only was he blessed with Broadway-worthy vocal talent, he was exceedingly good-looking with a bounty of blonde hair, sparkly blue eyes, and an Olympian physique. His performance would rain down sunshine on the audience and capture the hearts of the celebrity judges. Jeffrey was not telegenic, but he believed that his dark brown eyes and somber demeanor reflected the gravitas of a deep thinker. There was *pas de question* he would conquer the minds of the scholars on the panel with his exquisite rendering of the Bae Hyejin poems "I Meet You from Where I Am Not," "Only Stars See the Night," and "Freedom Is a Life Sentence." The renowned poetess herself had coached him in cadence. She'd selected a cerulean *hanbok* for him to wear and hired a dancer to teach him how to make the long sleeves appear to float on their own.

After a commercial break, the host would join the foreigners for the conversation segment of the competition. The first question would be the well-worn icebreaker: Do you prefer the mountains or the ocean? Those who favored the mountains were reflective introverts; people who preferred the ocean were adventurous extroverts. Jeffrey would describe a transformative experience he had amidst autumn foliage — colors unique to Korea — on a hike in Soraksan Mountain. Brig would say something like "Nothing makes me feel more alive than the ocean waves of Korea's stunning Haeundae Beach!" with a smile so dazzling the audience would rub their eyes.

The host would pull conversation starters from a list of stock questions: What makes Korea unique? What is your purpose in Korea? What is the organization of your siblings? Viewers would be glued to their televisions that night, fascinated to hear the mother tongue streaming out of the mouths of these exotic Western creatures. *March of Happiness* was expected to top the ratings.

Both men had an extraordinary aptitude for language acquisition. Brig had studied Korean at the Missionary Training Center in Provo, Utah, one of the best language training institutes in the world, before his mission to convert the natives of the Hermit Kingdom to The Church of Jesus Christ of Latter-day Saints. Jeffrey had taught himself how to read Korean before he left the States and had graduated at the top of his class from Yonsei University Korean Language Institute in Seoul. He composited an ever-expanding binder with a section for aphorisms. When Korea's historical misfortunes came up in conversations, "When whales fight, shrimp get crushed" said it all.

As the bus ran its route, thoughts of Brig alternated with thoughts of Sleeping Man. He'd be in the audience, wide awake, awestruck by Jeffrey's unsurpassable talents. After the show, he'd be waiting outside the studio for Jeffrey—who'd come out with trophy in hand. They would look into each other's eyes and *just know* they were meant for each other and walk together into the purity of the winter air.

The daydreaming ended when the bus passed the Moffet English Language Institute, where he'd been awarded Best Teacher of the Year. He realized with a gasp that he'd long ago missed his stop. The schedule of relaxing activities!

His anxiety abated when the bus pulled up to the next stop. He would grab a taxi home, never mind the cost. He'd play the exercises from *The Flutist's Formalae* by Georges Barrère. Or would he fiddle with the jigsaw puzzle of *Bridge over a Pond of Water Lilies*? He wouldn't have time for both now that he was behind schedule. He'd make that decision in the cab.

Sleeping Man and Beret Girl got off and ducked into a café. Jeffrey had spent one hour and fifteen minutes at the most serene café in Seoul that morning, where he'd written a letter to his sister about the travails of living in a land where nothing started on time. He'd written in his journal, and he'd allowed his thoughts to roam freely. The final words he'd penned was a Jean-Paul Sartre quote that expressed his own sentiments *exactement*: "If you are lonely when you're alone, you are in bad company." He felt a sudden need for coffee.

The café was run-down. The proprietor was wedging a wad of paper under the leg of a wobbly table. A lone kerosene heater did little to provide heat. People kept their coats on, drawing on cigarettes and exhaling streams of smoke dense with the condensation of cold air.

A group of men perked up as Sleeping Man approached their table. Beret Girl turned her head and smiled at Jeffrey. His face flushed red when he realized she'd known all along that he'd been following them. She walked up to the awkward American frozen at the door. Everybody in the café was looking at the round-eyed foreigner.

"*Hello. How are you? I am fine. Will you like coffee together?*" she said in English. Jeffrey was startled by her daring—approaching a stranger, a man, a foreigner—but he was also disarmed by her kind, melodious voice.

"It would be an imposition," he said in Korean.

"You speak Korean!" She was shocked—nothing that he hadn't seen before.

"My Korean is poor. I have much to learn," he said, modesty being a virtue.

She giggled, covering her mouth with her hand, modesty being a woman's virtue.

"*My name is Lee Songhwa.*" She bowed.

"*My name is Jeffrey Brown.*" His calibrated his bow to be a degree higher than hers.

"*Are American?*"

"*Yes. I'm an English teacher.*"

"*Mr. Jeffrey, come coffee with us.*"

If it weren't for the bus fiasco he'd be at home relaxing, but her insistent smile pulled him like a tugboat to the table where Sleeping Man sat. The conversation there stopped when they saw the Caucasian.

As often happened when Jeffrey was nervous, he started blinking rapidly, and not just because of Sleeping Man. It was the sight of the men: long hair past their shoulders, louche jeans, and an air of insouciance about them. These were rock and roll musicians; unemployment was their pastime. Jeffrey sympathized with those persecuted by the military dictatorship—intellectual dissidents, student activists, labor organizers—but rock and roll musicians were another story. The government branded them as a corrupting influence on young people. Jeffrey thought they could spare themselves trouble from the law if they were less conspicuous. He imagined police in riot gear storming in, where they'd rough up the musicians before dragging them to the police station. What if he was also arrested for fraternizing with them? The day was losing all semblance of relaxation.

"This is Mr. Jeffrey Brown," Songhwa said. "He's an English teacher from America—and he speaks our language!"

A huge man, twirling a drumstick, said, "Have the big-nose say something."

Jeffrey had never heard "big-nose" before, but it was clearly a put-down, bringing the heat of embarrassment to his face.

"Let's show him the best of Korean hospitality," she said. She placed her hand on Sleeping Man's shoulder. "This is my older brother Ritchie. He plays the guitar." Sister, she's his sister. Ritchie remained in his seat and nodded in acknowledgement, without a trace of interest. He was inscrutable, a trait Koreans seemed to cultivate especially for Westerners.

The others also did not stand up. Roger, the slack-jawed bass player, had long bangs over his sleepy eyes. Jon played a Hammond organ; he wore expensive clothes and smoked a slender cigarette with studied elegance. The drummer, whom she introduced as Big Ian, had frizzy hair that amplified his enormous build. Small Ian was the vocalist; he was a small man, shy, and seemed rather nice.

"It-it is an honor to meet you," Jeffrey said, bowing deeply, as if to make a point.

Big Ian grabbed a chair from another table and shoved Roger over to make room for Jeffrey—directly across from Ritchie. At any moment, embarrassment would present itself with the blinking or blushing, but nothing happened. His heart swelled instead.

"Say something else in Korean," Big Ian said.

He struggled to think of something interesting to say but started to get dizzy.

The drummer hurtled out of his chair and threw his drumsticks high up in the air, catching them behind his back when they came back down. "Now show me what you can do. Speak

Korean." His voice boomed to all corners of the café.

"Lower your voice," Ritchie said. His rich, resonating voice was comforting. Jeffrey no longer felt dizzy.

"Please say something in Korean," Big Ian whispered.

"Your-your . . . " What was the word for *drumsticks*? "That was very impressive."

"Impressive? That's a big word for a big-nose."

"Dear fat Ian, shut thy trap," Jon said. "Your manners are appalling."

"Dear skeleton Jon, who can't play shit, give us more money," Big Ian said.

Jon waved him off with an imperious gesture. He pulled out a silver cigarette case from his polished leather bag and scrutinized Jeffrey. "What brings you to this dilapidated establishment?"

"I-I came to meet a friend, but on the wrong day." He blushed with shame, for lying was against his nature. "I deeply apologize for interrupting your important discussion. It is disrespectful, so I shall remove myself from your honorable presence."

"Mr. Jeffrey here is more deferential than the most obsequious Korean," Jon said, flicking cigarette ash off his designer jeans.

"Stay, Mr. Jeffrey. You were going to spend time with your friend anyway," Songhwa said.

The proprietor came over with a tray of coffee in cups that had seen the erosion of time. The first time Jeffrey had had Korean-style coffee, he'd almost gagged. In the affluent homes of his private students, it was served in dainty porcelain cups and saucers. Politeness had forced him to ingest the syrupy blend of instant coffee, sugar, and powdered non-dairy creamer, and eventually he grew to like it.

"This stuff'll get you high if you drink enough of it," Roger said.

"Jon, mind if we have another round?" Big Ian said. Without waiting for a response, he called out for more coffee.

"Americans are a curious lot," Jon said. "You use the word

love for anything that you find pleasant. *I love ice cream! I love that color!*" He paused for effect. "We use that word sparingly, so it doesn't lose its value."

Jon's pontificating was subtracting time from the schedule of relaxing activities. Jeffrey stood up. "I-I apologize, but I must take my leave."

"Stay awhile," Ritchie said, easy and relaxed, as he reached for a cigarette. He struck a match. He looked at Jeffrey, less inscrutable than before, perhaps even with a hint of interest.

"OK" glided out of Jeffrey's mouth, and he sat back down.

"Please say something in Korean again. You're impressive," Big Ian said.

"Wh-why do you have English names?"

"We are the Korean counterpart to Deep Purple," Jon said. "You know, the English band." He surveyed Jeffrey's appearance. "I don't suppose you listen to heavy metal."

Jeffrey blinked.

"Apparently not."

"Cut the sarcasm," Ritchie said.

Jeffrey looked at Ritchie, who looked back with a flicker of interest. Self-conscious, he looked straight down. As he took a sip of coffee, he felt overcome with regret—if he'd sustained eye contact with Ritchie, the flicker could have grown into a flame.

"I'll answer your question," Small Ian said. "We take the names of the musicians by the instruments we play. I'm 'Ian' because I'm the singer for our band, just like Ian Gillian is for Deep Purple. Then there's Ritchie Blackmore, Jon Lord, Roger Glover, and Ian Paice."

"And etcetera. You get the picture," Jon said.

"No offense, but you're not cool," Big Ian said.

Humiliation flooded Jeffrey's face. He was too embarrassed to feel indignation. He'd read every existentialist novel, had translated a book on charcuterie from French to English, and had written an admired paper about the French restoration of Angkor

9

Wat. Yet, he was not "cool" because he wasn't familiar with heavy metal music. All one needed to know about the genre was that it was loud and discordant. He didn't look like them. His sister had said that he dressed like a wallflower because he didn't want to draw attention to himself. His short, tidy haircut went well with his Timex watch. He wore a brown crewneck sweater over a white button-down shirt, and he'd passed the iron over the crease of his brown slacks three times that morning.

"He's cool to me," Songhwa said.

"Let's not get off-topic," Jon said. "Let me explain. We coexist with Deep Purple in a parallel universe." He smoothed the contours of his glossy hair. "We are Deep Nirvana, not that nirvana has dimensions, but you get the picture."

"You're killing us with your brilliance, but let's talk about the gig," Ritchie said.

The band lost interest in their American novelty as they became absorbed with plans for that night's performance. Songhwa left to get cigarettes and ginseng energy drinks. Jeffrey reviewed the schedule of relaxing activities.

He wouldn't be fifteen minutes early as planned, but he'd be on time for a one-hour dinner with Amélie at a Japanese restaurant. She'd talk about her fiancé, Jacques-Louis, the French cultural attaché who detested Korea. After dinner, Jeffrey would escort Amélie to her residence and walk the full half hour home to observe the sound of snow crunch under his feet. There was a long bath scheduled at 8:45 p.m. with Chopin's nocturnes emanating from his high-fidelity turntable. At 9:15, he'd be in the armchair reading *Les Mots*. At 10:15, he'd tuck himself into bed and fall asleep to pleasant dreams under the perfect weight of the electric blanket his mother had sent him for Christmas.

He'd jump out of bed the next morning at 5:30 a.m. with confidence and vigor. The morning's schedule included stretching, meditation, breakfast, and a brisk walk. There was the dress rehearsal before his full-length mirror. At 9:15, he'd take a call-taxi to the studio, arriving fifteen minutes early. The studio would come alive with lighting technicians and set decorators buzzing about. The PAs would escort audience members to their designated seats and start audience participation drills. The host would don a sparkling suit and join Jeffrey and Brig at the makeup station. At 11:30 a.m., the cameras would start rolling to tape the show for that evening's prime time broadcast.

It was now forty minutes since Jeffrey had stepped into the café. His underarms were damp with the distinct odor of stress. If he did not resume the schedule of relaxing activities *tout de suite*, he might not sleep well that night, causing him to stumble through the poems and stammer in the conversation segment. Scrambled words ran laps around his head.

Roger went to the bathroom. He decided that he would go after Roger; instead of returning to the table — he'd leave.

The bathroom's aluminum door was misaligned. It screeched open to the sight of a squat toilet. He directed a steady stream of urine to the far reaches of the latrine, into the bullseye of its recess. He placed toilet paper on the flushing pedal before stepping on it. He looked into the mirror. Creases ran races across his forehead, and there was a mustache of sweat above his lip. Is this what Ritchie saw? *Oh, Ritchie.* He squeezed his eyes shut. *Ritchie was an accident.*

He looked back to see if anybody was watching him walk to the front door of the café. It felt bold to leave without saying goodbye. Just as he opened the door, Songhwa stepped in, accompanied by a gust of cold air.

"Are you leaving?" She looked forlorn.

"I was stepping out for throat lozenges." He lied without hesitation.

"The owner has ginger tea in the back."

"Goodbye!" He fled out the door.

Jeffrey checked his watch. He'd left the café twenty-seven minutes ago yet not a single taxi had come his way. He had no choice but to go back to the very bus stop that had led to the café episode.

"Hey, it's Mr. Cool!" Big Ian pulled up; he was at the wheel of a beat-up car jam-packed with his drum set, disassembled in a configuration of contiguous parts.

"Pretty impressive, right?" Big Ian grinned. "Jon, who can't play shit, has an 'assistant' who hauls his organ around in a trailer." He looked in the rearview mirror. "There he is." He hit the accelerator to shoot up, then slammed the brakes to a hard stop, making the car lurch back and forth.

Jon cruised up to the curb in a gleaming luxury sedan. Ritchie was in the passenger seat, with Roger, Songhwa, and Small Ian in the back.

Jon rolled down the window. "Surely you haven't been waiting for us all this time?"

"No, why, well—"

"Come with us, Mr. Jeffrey!" Songhwa said.

"Would you mind taking me to Shinsa-dong?"

"Whatever the American wants," Jon said.

They drove around the barbed-wire perimeter of Yongsan Garrison, the U.S. military base, and were soon on Itaewon's main thoroughfare.

Jeffrey had been to Itaewon once with his cousin, who'd come to Korea to pack her largest suitcase with name-brand sports shoes—Nike, Adidas, Converse, Reebok—that were the latest craze in the States. Around-the-clock factory labor supplied the demand; shops in Itaewon sold them at bargain-basement prices; and she made a handsome profit reselling them back in the U.S.

Deep Nirvana drove past a multitude of shops on the main drag that catered to Americans to the tail end, where a cluster of nighttime establishments provided R & R for American soldiers stationed at the base. The two cars maneuvered into a tight lot behind a club called NCO. The band loaded in the equipment, a slow and complicated process, while Jeffrey and Songhwa stood on the sidelines. A third car came along, towing a tiny trailer, and twisted its way into the lot.

"Miss Songhwa, why wasn't I taken to Shinsa-dong?"

"Mr. Jon wanted to get here before his organ did."

How little respect they had for him! Jeffrey ran from the back lot, to the sidewalk in front of NCO, and into the arms of an erratic traffic jam. The babel of asynchronous honking rattled him to the very core of his being. He pressed his palms against his ears, cultivated to listen to the great masterworks of the classical repertoire, or birdsong in a bucolic setting. He perched himself on the curb, stretched the length of his body upward, and waved his arms SOS-style.

"You'll never get a taxi."

He was aghast to see Songhwa. "Please let me be! I must get back to my schedule of relaxing activities!"

"A schedule?" She giggled.

"Yes, a schedule—oh, you wouldn't understand."

"Look," she said, pointing to an impasse up ahead.

Two taxi drivers were in a fistfight, their stranded passengers screaming. An earnest young policeman jumped in.

Jeffrey managed to flag a taxi, but an overweight American couple, sweating with aggression and clutching bursting shopping bags, cut in. The driver clucked in disapproval, but with the traffic picking up, it was easier to let the biggest and meanest get their way.

Jeffrey grabbed his head with his hands and stomped his feet, his face bursting in wretched defeat. Or perhaps he was angry. Time was collapsing around him.

He pulled himself together.

"I will be on *March of Happiness* tomorrow in a competition for the Korean Language Achievement Award."

"That ridiculous show? Really?" She laughed, a little too loud for a woman.

"Why do you make fun of me? This is a prestigious award! Please, Miss Songhwa, ask someone to take me home. I must relax!"

"We can do that while the band is warming up. When they perform, Deep Nirvana will take you to nirvana — where you will experience relaxation like never before."

"I cannot relax to rock and roll music. I'm not like you."

Songhwa tilted her head to the side. "My brother would like it if you stayed."

"Did-did he say so?"

She smiled. "More or less." Then she was dead-on serious: "Itaewon is the only place where my brother's band can play without getting busted by the police. American soldiers can get away with anything in Itaewon."

He suddenly remembered that he hadn't called Amélie. He ran into NCO. It was dim inside; the house lights were not on yet. A youth sorted beers below the bar as the bartender arranged glasses next to bottles of Johnny Walker on the shelf above. A girl placed napkins in the hollows of translucent ashtrays and saturated them with water for putting out cigarettes. Hostesses sat in the shadows, smoking and applying extra layers of lipstick.

The manager, attired in all-black with a red sequined bow tie, walked around the club making spot checks. He took the panic-stricken civilian to a rotary phone. In his haste, Jeffrey failed to dial the finger wheel all the way to the metal stop. He called the wrong number. He spoke in French when he called the Japanese restaurant. By the time Amélie was on the line, he had lost all composure. She was always there for him, soothing frazzled nerves, listening patiently to his complaints.

Yes, the film was just as thought-provoking as she'd said, but then the day had turned into a complete disaster. He was at a disreputable place in Itaewon with heavy metals. She asked why he was carrying around heavy metals. When he rephrased it, she told him that listening to unfamiliar music expanded the mind. She assured him there was ample time for the remaining relaxing activities. And not to worry — she hadn't eaten alone — Jacques-Louis had insisted on coming because they had run out of cheese.

After the call, Jeffrey was making his way through an obstacle course of tables — when Big Ian came flying out of nowhere.

"Mr. Cool!" He zipped up his fly. "Songhwa's been looking for you."

"Well, tell her I left," Jeffrey said, with a toss of his head.

"We can't let you leave without supper." Big Ian dragged him to the rehearsal space where Songhwa was eating *jja-jjang myun* noodles. He plunked down a bowl for Jeffrey, and she slid over side dishes of kimchi, pickled turnip, and raw onion.

Ritchie was with Jon when he saw Jeffrey. "Don't forget to take the lead for the outro," he told Jon, before walking over to Jeffrey, who was struggling to mix black bean sauce with the noodles.

"You're back," Ritchie said, taking the bowl and chopsticks from him.

As Ritchie wound sauce around the noodles, Jeffrey imagined the apparition of love rays beaming from the musician's heart. Ritchie's voice was resounding, golden, heartwarming . . . he would write these words in his journal under the column header "Vocal Qualities."

"I appreciate you keeping my sister company."

"Oh, yes," Jeffrey said, shaking himself from the melody of words he was composing.

"And re-lax." Ritchie handed the noodles back to him, with the hint of a smile. "You might even enjoy yourself."

Ritchie went back to work. Was he flirting when he said "you might even enjoy yourself?" Amélie had once said that love is spontaneous. Perhaps it was time for an impromptu. He would replace the next two relaxing activities on his schedule with one of the same duration: "Observation of rock and roll ('heavy metal') culture." If he got home by 10:15, he'd have time for a quick bath, pushing bedtime to 10:30. This would require removing one activity from the morning schedule.

Jeffrey took mental notes as he watched Deep Nirvana warm up. With their instruments, they were different. Roger wasn't a numbskull. Big Ian was subdued. Jon seemed almost humble. Small Ian was unflinching. Ritchie wasn't casual — he was engrossed, intense, passionate . . . Jeffrey's starry-eyed gaze elicited a distracted glance from Ritchie.

"Did you hear me?" Songhwa said.

"Pardon?"

"Ritchie just got a guitar called *Fen-der Strat-o-caster*. Jon bought it and had it smuggled into the country. Ask him about it."

"Oh, no. I don't want to ruin his concentration."

Songhwa got up and whispered something into Ritchie's ear. He nodded and sauntered over to Jeffrey, who slowly rose to his feet.

"You're into guitars?" Ritchie said.

"Well, I did have my Segovia period."

"A classical guitar would improve my technique." He held up the Stratocaster. "For now, this will do."

The guitar had a variety of fixtures attached to it. Jeffrey examined three descending dials on the body of the instrument.

"This is the volume control, and these two are tone controls," Ritchie said. "Let's try something. I'll play a riff, and you handle the tone controls."

Jeffrey turned a control and the pitch soared. Ritchie wrapped his fingers around Jeffrey's and guided the control the other way. His touch was warm and gentle. His eyes roved over Jeffrey's face for a brief moment, then just as quickly his attention shifted to working the strings of his guitar.

Jeffrey went back to Songhwa.

"I saw that," she said.

"Saw what?" His heart was pounding.

The manager trod quietly to the band. They put their instruments on pause and followed him to a hidden door in the back. It was black, seamless with the nightclub's black walls. Jon handed an envelope to the manager, who made it disappear from sight. He unbolted a padlock and walked away. Jon led the group up a free-standing metal staircase that shook with each step.

At the top of the stairs, Jon reached under the floor of the roof access enclosure and pulled out a manila envelope, which contained a magazine. He crouched on the floor and assembled an apparatus with parts from his bag. Roger was first. The odor of cannabis drifted down the stairway. Jeffrey turned to flee — only to face the girth of Big Ian.

"Are you scared?"

He wasn't going to be taunted again. He turned back around and saw Roger walk out the door to the roof. Before him was a smoldering needle standing upright on its cardboard base. An inverted glass was next to it. Jon nudged a chip of the cannabis onto the point of the needle.

"Is this your first time?" Jon asked. "Use this straw to inhale the smoke when I tilt the glass. Don't exhale until you're out on the roof."

Jon lit the chip, then blew out the flame and placed the glass over the apparatus. Smoke filled the glass like a blinding fog. Jon tilted the glass. Jeffrey hesitated.

"Do it," said Big Ian.

Jon tilted the glass again. Jeffrey slid the straw under the glass and inhaled. He joined Roger on the roof, where he had a coughing fit. When everyone came out, they formed a huddle against the enclosure from the bone-chilling wind that swept over the roof.

"This is the shit!"

"What is it?"

"How'd you get it?"

"Hashish. From France. Flattened, wrapped in aluminum foil, inserted into a magazine, sent via diplomatic pouch." Jon took a drag of his cigarette. "I have connections."

Ritchie said, "Time to get back to work."

"Let me go in first," Jon said. "I'll dispense blessings once more."

NCO was filling up with U.S. servicemen. Big belt buckles against taut abdomens, crisp jeans fresh out of the laundry, name-brand sports shoes just off the rack. T-shirts emblazoned with logographs of rock bands. The soldiers were all smiles and ready to kick ass.

Songhwa led Jeffrey to a table that had just been wiped down.

"Don't you feel good?" she said, her head arched back.

He was in a rocket ready for lift off to the far reaches of the universe. He was also on a spiral staircase without handrails.

A hostess with a mountain of teased hair came to their table. *"What you like?"* An irradiated color wheel whirled around her hair. Wasn't it dark just a minute ago?

"We like drink," Songhwa said in English.

"You look too innocent to be in a place like this," the hostess said in Korean. "Did your boyfriend take you away from your homework?"

"She's not my girlfriend," Jeffrey said. *"I'm just a tagalong."* He talked as slow as molasses.

"OK, Ta-gal-ong, what you drink?"

"Water, make it Michigan water."

"No Mi-chi-gan. Only Korean water. And. This is booze place."

A drunk soldier took a seat and ordered a drink for Jeffrey: a big fat mug full of frothy amber liquid, a shot glass lurking within. He lifted his mug to make a toast, but Jeffrey sat motionless.

"What'sa matter?"

"I want to go home."

"Well, you can't." He had a motorcycle smile. *"Wanna know what I'm thinkin'?"* He downed his drink. *"I'm cruisin' for a bruisin'. With a friendly guy like you."*

Jeffrey was not thinking very clearly but he understood two things: he didn't want to drink, and if he didn't drink this big soldier was going to hurt him.

Songhwa pulled Jeffrey's sweater. "It's just one beer."

Jeffrey picked up the mug.

A hand reached down and lifted Jeffrey up from the puddle of vomit his face was in.

"*Hey, buddy, you OK?*"

He was propped up against the bathroom wall. The friendly voice wiped gunk off his face.

"*There you go, fresh as a peach.*"

"*Pardon?*"

"*You still out of it, bud?*"

He nodded.

"*Well then, let's help you get back to your table.*"

He followed the lanky private through a tangle of drinking games, chest-thumping, and dancing. On the stage was a group of first sergeants performing "(I Can't Get No) Satisfaction." He was no longer drunk, but the effects of hashish remained.

"Over here!" Songhwa waved.

The private gave Jeffrey a pat on the shoulder. "*Take care, bud.*"

Songhwa frowned with concern. "Do you feel better?"

He thought about it. "Yes, much better." Vomiting had not only purged evil toxins from his body, it had quelled the weight of anxiety that had been second nature to him.

She smiled with delight. "You're ready for Deep Nirvana."

"As long as it's not too deep, wouldn't want to get lost."

Her laughter blended in with whoops and finger whistles when Deep Nirvana came onstage. With their long, unruly hair and renegade jeans, the musicians were vicarious versions of the soldiers who'd left their uniforms and regimented lives behind at the military base that night.

The band gripped their instruments, ready to go. Ritchie

played the intro, a commanding guitar riff, joined by Jon on organ and Big Ian on drums, followed by Roger's bassline, leading to Small Ian at the mic. Jeffrey listened to "Smoke On The Water" as a musicologist would and determined that it had aesthetic value. He liked the lyrics, a story about a fire in a casino, that is, until he heard: "But Swiss time was running out/It seemed that we would lose the race." Was this a message that he'd lose to Brig, now that he'd lost track of time?

His anxiety dissipated when Ritchie began his solo. His eyes were closed. He had extreme focus, while traveling in another world. When he tilted his head back in ecstasy, a shimmering rainbow encircled him like a halo. The rainbow became a spinning wheel, revolving at time-lapse speed, propelling threads off the stage. The threads wove themselves into an undulating blanket that floated over to Jeffrey, settling its featherweight warmth around his shoulders. He felt an abundance of affection for everyone: young men lost in riotous laughter, sassy hostesses slapping men's hands, the glittering red bow tie bobbing about like a buoy. He was blitzed with glee, wriggling in sync to the distorted bends of Deep Nirvana.

A distant voice from the future reminded him of the competition the next day: Go home to relax — it's past bedtime. *Go away.* You're confusing enjoyment with relaxation. If you don't return to normalcy, Brig will win tomorrow. *That's in the future.* Tomorrow is the future, you idiot. Enough! No more excuses.

Jeffrey slapped his cheeks bright red.

"What's wrong?" Songhwa said.

He sagged in his chair and said in English: "*I lack the wherewithal to ascertain what a relaxing activity is.*"

She touched his face. "Don't worry. You're in nirvana."

He rested his head on the table in the cradle of his arms. All the merriment had taxed him. His eyes felt heavy, and to unburden them, he fell asleep.

"Wake up! It's curfew time!" Songhwa shook Jeffrey's shoulder. They ran outside, and everyone piled into Jon's car. Songhwa sat on Ritchie's lap. Big Ian pushed Roger and Jeffrey over to squeeze in. As soon as Small Ian hopped onto Big Ian's lap, Jon hit the gas.

Buses had stopped running. Strangers crammed into the few cabs still out on the streets. A siren sounded in the distance, a warning to those breaking curfew.

"Roger, Ian, and Ian stay at my place," Jon said. "Mr. Jeffrey, you're on the other side of town, so we can't take you home."

"You'll stay with us," Songhwa said.

Jeffrey tried to weigh the consequences of not going home. He couldn't think of any.

They crossed the Han River and drove through a vast commercial district where neon lights, scintillating when on, were now dead. They turned onto a well-paved street that led to a luxury apartment complex. Jon greeted the security guard at the gate and dropped Roger and the two Ians off at his building.

Jon gripped the steering wheel with both hands and drove with steady speed. The number of streetlights diminished as the distance from the city increased. They got off the freeway, where it veered off into farmland, and traveled up a narrow road that led to a dimly lit townlet. Jon slowed to a crawl over a series of potholes. The final destination was a small apartment building from a past era, before Seoul's factories and manufacturing plants had emptied the countryside.

Ritchie and Songhwa waited outside while Jeffrey reached around for his bag.

"Is it safe for you to drive back?" Jeffrey said.

"My father is one of the richest men in Korea, and I'm his only son." Jon was deadpan. "Besides, the police don't mind taking donations." Before driving off, he said to Ritchie: "Older brother, thank you for including me."

It was the smallest home Jeffrey had ever seen. It was tidy and spotless. The walls had yellowed like the pages of an old paperback. A second-hand TV and other comforts of home lined a bench draped in a vinyl tablecloth.

Two squealing adolescent girls came out of the bedroom and jumped on their brother, who then played dead. Songhwa pried them off and took them back to bed.

Ritchie remained on the floor in repose. Jeffrey heard a torrent of water running in the bathroom. He went over and watched Songhwa turn off the faucet of a brimming bathtub; pajamas and a toothbrush were on the toilet seat. He pulled her back in as she was leaving. He was confused: the bathtub would overflow when he got in. She told him to stand outside of the tub and to fill the bath bucket with water to lather and rinse. Now he knew why Korean bathroom floors had drains. She gave him a reassuring smile and closed the door. He tore his clothes off, inside out—something he never did—so eager was he to wash off the miasma of that night's revelry.

Ritchie broke out in laughter when he saw Jeffrey. The pajama pants bunched up at the crotch and the shirt pinched his underarms. It was deeply embarrassing to be an object of amusement for the object of affection.

"I'm sorry my pajamas are too small for you," Ritchie said.

"No, it's my fault they don't fit."

"You're funny, the way you speak Korean."

Jeffrey forced a nonchalant laugh.

"Should we rip the seams open?"

"Oh?"

"Or should my sister make you a pair on her sewing machine?"

"Hmm."

"Or should you sleep naked?"

"They say it's better for your health." There. Repartee.

"We'll figure something out." Ritchie sprung to his feet to wash up.

Jeffrey looked at the bedding Songhwa had laid out: two *yo* floor mattresses, with comforters and cylindrical pillows. Were the *yos* too close to each other, or not close enough? What a foolish thought! A man as beautiful as Ritchie would have to be desperate to be with him—he who had once been mocked for being the worst lay ever. Better to avoid it altogether, pretend to be asleep.

Ritchie flicked the light off on his way back from the bathroom. Jeffrey listened to every detail of him getting into bed. Flipping the comforter over to get in. Pulling it over himself. Rustling around. Throwing his head on the pillow. Then it was quiet.

"Are you asleep?"

Jeffrey snored pleasantly.

"Are you pretending?"

"Wh-what?"

In a swift second, Ritchie planted a wet, messy kiss on Jeffrey's mouth. He recoiled. The kiss was a malodorous brew of cigarettes, black bean sauce, beer, kimchi, pickled turnip, and raw onion.

"Sorry, I forgot to brush my teeth."

Ritchie returned with a mint-fresh breath.

The two men lay in silence. Ritchie cleared his throat.

"How are you doing?"

"Very well. Songhwa is talented at making beds."

Ritchie laughed. What was it now?

"Did you like the music?"

"Oh, yes. I'm a big fan of Deep Nirvana."

"It's a relief to shed Ritchie's skin."

"What's your Korean name?"

"Dongho."

"Can I call you Dongho?"

"I'd like that." He propped himself on his elbow. "Do you have another name?"

"Just a nickname my family calls me: Jeffy."

"Jeffy," Dongho said before he kissed Jeffrey, this time slow and tender.

Dongho had fallen asleep right away, but Jeffrey had lain awake all night, trying to make sense of that day's chaos. It all seemed to lead to being with Dongho, deliciously naked. He reached for his watch. It was 5:30 a.m.; his alarm was beeping at home. He forced himself to think about the unavoidable — the competition that had so consumed him. He canceled the schedule of morning activities. Better to get a few hours of sleep in the familiarity of his own bed. His suit and tie were already laid out, and the *hanbok* was in the closet fresh from the dry cleaner.

He went to the bathroom to relieve himself. He was horrified by the monstrous stubble he saw in the mirror — his face had been fertilized by vomitus. Before he put his soiled clothes on, he turned his boxers outside in, then inside out.

The bedding looked as if a storm had swept through. He folded his bedding. He sat on the floor and watched Dongho sleep. He placed his hand over his heart — it was palpitating with preemptive heartache. He considered leaving a note but dreaded the likelihood that the phone would never ring. It'd happened before. He told himself that instead he would go club-hopping in Itaewon, sometime in the future, to listen to rock and roll.

It was dark and quiet outside, and the winter air was crisp and refreshing. He didn't know where a bus stop was, and it might be a long wait before a bus came. He couldn't find a sidewalk. He wondered how long the morning twilight would last. As he trudged on the ground crackling with ice, he realized the pressure to win was gone. The only thing he could predict about the future was Brig's victory.

HOW THE LIGHT HITS

The trees are facing north. North
is where you are tonight, thoughts

of me escaping your head like recess
children. Here I am walking by my

own side down a street where even the moon,
big and whole as it is, can only light one side

of the trees. That's the thing about being
everywhere. It can't be done.

When you were here, together we were a lightplanet.
We could fan out and shine up the street. Even

cat's eyes, sudden emeralds, would show up from
under parked cars. But now, the moon

does what it can, and who can blame it?
The moon, after all, is only human.

STRANIERA

Two years into exile and still waiting
to fall into place, feel at home
in a thong, won't venture out
to where she can't touch,
heads daily to the beach
like homework, wades through

a bronzed sea
of bodies splayed
under the late-summer *Ferragosto* sun.
Tanned breasts,
pursed at the tips,
pull languidly to the sides, like half-filled
leather bags. She looks for an empty patch
of beach, the size of a janamaz,
spreads her towel,
lies back. Luxurious bodies

of clouds stretch
in white marble gestures,
like Venus crouching
at her bath. She rolls

onto her belly, reaches behind
to undo the strap,
pulls the bikini top from under, firmly presses

her breasts into the heat, takes a moment
to feel the burn of transgression
before turning to bare
sandy nipples to the world

though no one is looking,
no cup-bearer waiting
for a sacrificial offering of a swim top,
no Roman rite of passage to brave.

Clouds carry on, some cut across, upstage each other.
A low one casts a modest shade,
festooned over her like a washed chador
fetched from a line.

"All you have to do is give me the earrings."

JENNIFER SAVRAN KELLY

THE ELEVATOR

I press the button for the seventh floor. Not because it's my job—though I never can escape the idea that I'm here to serve—but because I'm plagued by the troublesome feeling I know this traveler who's been coming and going to and from the seventh floor, that perhaps we're even close friends or sisters or lovers. A vexing thing about living in the elevator is that I don't remember much from day to day. For the most part it's only details, tidbits, and only if they repeat, so I revel in remembering when I can. In this case, the details of the traveler to the seventh floor: their red hair and dark eyes, the shine of their shoes, the number seven. Their smile, which seems genuine, and the one front tooth that's slightly shorter than the rest. But if we've spoken or when, I can't say. Nor if we've touched, though that's unlikely because one of the unspoken rules I've observed during my limitless time in the elevator is that touching rarely occurs, not between lovers or friends or parents and children. For such a small space, an elevator creates more distance between people than any other.

The elevator is my home, at least it has been for as long as I can remember. I call it an *elevator* because it's easier than calling it *eternity*. An elevator is easy to picture; it has shape and purpose. From what I can tell, my elevator is in a hotel, and its decor is decidedly art deco—green velvet walls, bordered with dark, intricately carved wood, a mirror on the wall, which lets me see myself when I want to, and a checkered marble floor. The whole thing is about twenty-two square feet and adequately lit.

Everyone has exited now except the person from the seventh floor, who offers me their kind smile. I hope they don't catch me studying them, trying to piece back together what I can aside from small, insignificant details. (I call everyone *them* because I can't remember a time when gender wasn't fluid—at least for me, if you can call this eternal, changeable being "me.") My eye catches the glint of the traveler's earring, and when they see me looking, their hand darts to their ear to cover it. I avert my eyes. The chime signals our arrival at the seventh floor, and they turn to leave without a word or another glance in my direction. I want to follow, but as I watch them step out of the elevator, something falls to the ground. One of the earrings.

"You've dropped something," I say.

They stop in the doorway. "Thank you."

Before I have a chance to pick it up for them, they bend down. But their hand only brushes the earring. They depart without it as the door closes.

I'm alone with the sense that something important has just occurred, but I can't remember what. I wish I'd gone after them, but whenever the elevator empties of travelers, before I can make it to the door, something deep inside tells me to stop. I lose all recollection of who I was before they left, replaced only by a strong sense that I'm now someone new. And I am.

Each time I change into a new person, I find myself holding, among other things, an object, or I find one in my pocket or purse— something that has been endowed with memories, practically a lifetime of them, to complete my new identity. I'm aware of this because there's a certain artificiality to the memories. They're as vivid as can be and their pull at my emotions is strong, but they don't feel like they belong to me; it's as if I know they're merely on loan.

This is the hardest thing—not being trapped for eternity in a place that doesn't let me arrive with the other travelers, but not knowing who I am or how I came to be here.

Already the details of the past few minutes have begun to recede—until my eye catches sight of an earring. I search my memory. Someone must have dropped it on their way out of the elevator. I try to remember who so that I can return it, but nothing surfaces. Then I pick it up, and something new happens. It takes a few breaths for me to understand. Holding the earring in my hand, new memories flood in, but the result is a kind of chaos in my heart and mind I've never experienced before; I'm paralyzed by emotion. Genuine emotion.

The chime signals and the number one illuminates, breaking my strange reverie. Just before the door opens, I drop the earring.

At the lobby, a family boards. New-comers, loaded down with suitcases and extra handbags. The mother nods politely in the way that says *hello* would take more resources than they can spare. I recognize the feeling, know it deep in my bones. But how? The kids in the elevator are all hands, jockeying for the button to bring them to the sixteenth floor. The parents shake their heads. "Bobby," says the father, and in an instant, stillness. I recognize this too, the relief that follows the quiet. It pulls at my heart. I want to comfort this young mother. But I don't know where these feelings are coming from, and it's making me dizzy. Mercifully, no one else boards. As soon as Bobby and his family exit, before the door closes and I begin to transform, I pick up the earring.

This time, even before I walk to the mirror, I recognize myself. With the earring in my hand, I know what face I'll find in the glass; it's a face I've had before. The earring, too, belongs to me. The mirror confirms it: I appear as female, blond, a small cap pinned in my hair. It's part of my maid's uniform, the one I wear while I clean this very hotel. I got the job after I left my family. It's coming back to me almost too fast to keep up. I had a husband and a daughter. The daughter a baby, needy and colicky, clinging to me day and night, shrieking every time she needed anything, nuzzling close when she slept. I can almost feel the weight of her on my hip. And my husband — Bernard — I feel the weight of him too. His hands on my shoulders like a lead blanket. He was a kind man with big, warm hands, hands that loved to touch me. When we'd met, I thought those hands were an asset. They seemed to stand for strength and protection, all of the things I was supposed to want. But as the days passed, those hands became grotesque, not because of anything Bernard did, but because they weighed me down. If it wasn't Tess pulling at my breast, it was Bernard gently smothering me. I could never get out from under that sensation. Hands everywhere, holding me down, keeping me. And of course there was no one you could talk to back then, whenever "then" was, no way to come up for air. There was only "supposed to." So one day I left. I didn't mean to stay away but hours turned into days, and I didn't know how to go back, what I'd say, if Bernard would have me. I only had enough cash for one or two nights in the hotel, so I offered to work. I gave a fake name, thinking I would only be another day or two, and then of course I would return. I thought for sure each day that I would see Bernard walk through the revolving door and that he would scoop me up and carry me home, to Tess, to his giant hands. But every day that passed was another day he didn't come, and after a little while I stopped expecting him and I assumed he'd stopped expecting me.

I didn't like working as a maid, but there were no choices. I wasn't qualified to teach or type. One night I was cleaning the room of a man who looked like Bernard, even the hands — strong and overwhelming. I don't know if I was too friendly because he reminded me of my husband or if he saw something in me, but one night, he was pouring himself a whiskey and offered to pour me one too. When I refused, he laughed and put the top back on the bottle. That was it. Not another word until the next night, when he offered me another glass and again I refused. For several nights it went on this way: offer, refusal, laughter. It seemed like a nice game, and I began to enjoy seeing him night after night.

"How long are you staying?" I asked. I wasn't allowed to talk to the patrons unless I was answering a question, but I'd been emboldened by his nightly offers of whiskey.

"Two more days," he said, holding up the bottle. He smiled, a lock of hair falling into his eye, which he brushed out of the way with the glass in his hand. "So, Ruth, you don't have much time left to take me up on my offer."

The hair on the back of my neck stood up. "How do you know my name?"

"When a man is interested, he has ways."

Despite my hesitation, and even fear of his advances, my body filled with heat.

"Don't look so scared," he said, laughing. "I asked at the front desk."

I couldn't speak.

"I can tell you want to," he said, taking off his suit jacket and folding it over the back of the desk chair. He put the bottle down and approached me by the garbage bin, which I was emptying. He took the bag from my hands and replaced it with the glass of whiskey.

"No," I said, even though he was right. I did want to. I shook my head no.

"Just one." He was close enough that I could smell his breath — potatoes and alcohol.

"I have to go," I said.

"Not until you finish cleaning. You still have the bathroom." A vein pumped eagerly in his neck, and I had to resist the urge to touch him.

I put the whiskey down and accidentally stepped on the garbage bag. Though there was nothing threatening about him, he scared me, or maybe it was my attraction to him that scared me.

"What's going on, Ruth?" he said. His confusion looked sincere. "Where are you going?"

I was already out of his room.

The next night I should have asked one of the other girls to clean his room, but the truth was I wanted to see him. When I got there, I expected him to reach for the bottle, and I even thought this time I might say yes, but he changed the routine. Instead of whiskey, he offered me a jewelry box.

What's this? I wanted to ask, but I knew what it was. A bribe. Payment. I said, "You've got nerve."

He looked offended. "Really, Ruth? That's how you to talk to someone who's offering you a gift?"

"I don't know what game you're playing —"

He grabbed my arm. "Me?" he said. I thought he was going to cry. "Who's the one playing games?"

"Need I remind you that you're the one who offers me a drink every night, despite my constant refusal?"

"I don't think you understand what you've started, Ruth," he said. He had a wild look in his eye.

Something about the way he kept saying my name made it sound like a warning. I wanted to leave, but he was blocking the doorway.

"You'll take the gift," he said.

"And if I don't?" My heart was beating in my throat. I wanted to scream, but I could barely speak.

Again he thrust the jewelry box toward me, and this time I took it out of fear of what he would do if I refused a second time. The gesture calmed him. He let out breath, brushed aside the lock of hair that had fallen back into eyes. He stepped partially out of the way and clasped his hands together.

"My apologies," he said. "I'm sorry I got so worked up." He reached for my cheek. Frozen, I let him hold my face in the palm of his big, warm hand. So strange how all at once the threat becomes the shelter. He bowed his head and took another step back, implying that I was permitted to leave.

As soon as I heard his door click closed behind me, I ran, leaving my cleaning cart in his room. I thought I would go to my boss and tell him what had happened, but how would I explain my part in it? It would only get me fired and make it impossible for me to find another job. When I got to the stairwell, I stopped.

The idea that he might come after me and trap me in there was too terrifying to imagine. I ran to the elevator and by some grace the door had just opened. A woman smiled and held it for me as I stepped inside. She looked well off, put together, like she knew something about success. But she smiled like she also knew something about working a service job. I don't know why but her presence settled me, at least enough that I let down my guard.

"You're crying," she said, as we waited for the elevator to begin its descent.

"Am I? I apologize." I wiped my eyes.

"Never apologize for your feelings," she said. "I'm just surprised. Lobby?"

I nodded.

"You're holding such a pretty box," she said. "What could make you so sad when surely someone special has given you a gift?"

I'd forgotten about the jewelry box. I jumped back like I'd discovered a dead animal in my hands.

The woman put a hand on my shoulder. "What's upsetting you?" she said. She looked at the box. Then she did something that startled me. She stopped the elevator.

"What are you doing?" Sweat bloomed under my arms.

"Are you in danger?"

Danger. It was the first time I'd considered that word. "I don't know."

"What's in the box?"

I looked up at her eyes, her perfectly put-on face. Somehow I knew she could help, though I couldn't put words to it. I opened the box. Sitting on top was a small photograph. It was Tess, my daughter. The photograph was taken through a window to my living room. She was sitting on the couch with her doll, pretending to give it a bottle, her fat little hand gripping tight, a concerned look on her face. She was bigger than I remembered.

The woman in the elevator stared at the photograph. "I don't understand," she said.

"I'm not sure I do either." I looked at my daughter again, not wanting to tear my eyes away, until I began to put together what was happening. My hands shaking, I turned the photograph over. I felt faint. Printed in dark blue ink was my home address. I thought about how he kept calling me Ruth—as if to show me he knew something about me. It was only the beginning. He'd found out where I lived. "Oh my god," I whispered. "He's threatening me."

"Who is?"

I held out the box. Beneath the photograph were two gold earrings. They looked like bows, with small diamond heart-shaped charms hanging from the center. I tried to draw breath, but I was shaking too hard, and soon my whole body racked with sobs. The woman took the box and opened her arms to me. I fell into them, breathed in her floral perfume, felt her chest rise and fall against mine. It was the most comfort I'd ever known. She held me for what felt like an eternity before she spoke.

"If you want, I can make him forget you," she whispered. "And your daughter."

I lifted my head, wiped my eyes. "What? How?"

"All you have to do is give me the earrings. Let me take them from the elevator before you leave." She handed the little case back to me.

"I don't understand."

"It's simple." She put her hand on my cheek. "You just have to do as I said. I promise."

I looked down at the photo of my daughter. Thought of the man's fat hand on my cheek, the odor of potato overwhelming my senses. Had I brought this on myself? Trapped myself in a terrible corner with a man who would threaten my family? Trapped myself in this elevator with a strange, beautiful woman? I wanted out. But I couldn't see the way.

"I promise," she said. Her hand hovered over the button to restart the elevator. "The choice is yours." She pressed the button and our little room jerked to life. She pulled a compact from her purse and examined herself in the tiny mirror as we descended. Within seconds the chime sounded. We'd arrived at the lobby. I had to think fast. I had nothing to lose. I didn't want the earrings anyway.

As the woman stepped toward the doors, she turned back to me. *Last chance.* I thought of that man's hands on my daughter. Wiping my eyes, I handed the woman the case with the earrings, and she accepted them. Then I waited, let the door close as she'd instructed.

And that's the last thing I remember about the person I've become. Now I'm back (still?) in the elevator, holding one of the earrings, one little gold bow with a rhinestone-heart charm. I don't know if the strange woman has just exited or if it was a hundred years ago. I can't sense time in the elevator. Afraid someone will board and leave, sparking me to change again, I press the button to stop my ascent. I need to time to understand what's happening — if I've discovered who I am or if it's another illusion. I have no way to know, aside from the fact that these memories feel like mine — not borrowed, not wholly dependent on my touching the earring — and this is the only person I've been who has an attachment to the hotel. Also, as far as I can remember, I came to possess this earring in an unusual way. The traveler from the seventh floor. How could I remember that? Was it possible they were my daughter? Or granddaughter? Were they the strange woman who'd taken my earrings?

Even in my confusion, my mind feels clearer than ever. I reach into the pockets of my apron and am not surprised to find the photograph of Tess. I take in her red curls, her chubby hand gripping the bottle, and tears rush in like centuries of pain. I'm heartbroken and scared, and I have nowhere to go, no way to know if my family is still alive or if they would want me back or even if I would want to go to them, no way to know if the man from the hotel is still out there ready to harm my daughter if I don't give him what he wants. I have no way to know if I'm real or if I can even leave the elevator. But if it's true that I got here by choice, there's only one way to find out if I can leave. Straightening my cap, I compose myself to the best of my ability and press the button to release the elevator. In a few seconds, the chime signals my arrival at the seventh floor. A stranger waits in the hallway, their head bowed. When they look up, I see tears in their eyes.

I step aside to allow them to board. I say, "Whatever it is, you're going to be all right. I believe I can help you."

ABSENT EVERYWHERE

She's been gone for little over a year.
He notices he's already begun to claim
theirs as his alone.

Like the old schnauzer she laughingly named
Useless, who now sleeps under the quilt on their —
his queen-size bed.

At the veterinarian's office he clears his throat,
swallows twice, before he can allow: Useless is our —
ahh, my dog.

He hesitates, takes a half breath before inviting
a friend to come visit this weekend up to, uh —
up to my camp.

He keeps wayward slips of tongue in his vest pocket,
like the threadbare handkerchief she used to fold
and tuck there.

He hoards each lapse as if finding a way
to rearrange them might fetch her back, mend
the tatters of his heart.

TWILL TIES

She stands in the small curtained cell,
silently bows her head to ask for help.
Stiff fingers no longer able to tie johnnies,
her eyes retreat to some remote chapter,
perhaps a savory page from her past,
a long-forgotten footnote.

The steadying hand she leans on me
lifts lightly as I ease her blouse over
porcelain shoulders, reach behind her
to undo her brassiere. She stands erect,
permits her skirt to fall, folds her things
quickly, stores them in the hospital locker.

Naked, she peeks at herself and shrugs;
laughing, we hug to hold each other up.

I know I was never supposed to see her like this;
exposed, glowing in her crêpe-de-chine,
mother-of-pearl, eighty-four-year-old skin,
a book of watermarked parchment,
foxed and bound by the inevitable.

She composes herself, slips into two gowns;
front to back, back to front, folds soft muslin
one edge over the other, smooths the overlap,
crosses her arms to embrace breasts and belly.

My glance sheers off, clings to the wall.
I draw the tapes around her waist, knot
my fear with twill ties.

THE GIRL WHO COULDN'T SEE HER TURQUOISE

within me 'tis as if
the green and climbing eyesight of a cat
crawled toward my mind's poor birds.
　　　　　　　　—Trumbull Stickney

I can't remember just where
I met the young woman with light wheat hair.
On a river path asking for directions? At a Marriott
breakfast bar in the fruit line? You know dreams.
Maybe I showed her to a stairway. I do recall,
with detail, her face—crusted
pimples at her mouth, sharp
worry-crease—but her voice was calm, even
a lilt, her step was steady.
She wore a vivid turquoise shirt,
a shout of blue into a June sky.

I could almost see it when she bent her head at times:
. . . *the green and climbing eyesight*—but then
that shiny ripple of terror blinked off, twisted
back into a girl's plain face.

Only when I admired her shirt and she looked up
did I see that her eyes were blasted, sad,
the grey crumbs of spent erasers.
She said *Oh . . . it has a color?*

I didn't know my shirt had a color.
I thought it was the color
of nothing.

Young, still lilting, but even
sound eyesight and turquoise near her heart
. . . crawls toward my mind's poor birds —
could not protect her.

*"People would fall in the water unexpectedly, or we'd
be juggling fire and I'd drop a club off stage."*

YOU WILL UNDERSTAND AFTER ENTERING

Casa Bonita as Sign of the Times

It's November 21st, and I'd expected the parking lot to be empty.

It's not, of course. It's a Saturday afternoon, 4:00 p.m., and patrons hustle between shops and restaurants — a Dollar Tree, a Burger King, a Planet Fitness. As a couple walks by my window, it occurs to me that I'd be able to see their breath if it weren't for their masks. They're holding hands, this couple, and I wonder about them: how long they've been together, if they come around this shopping center often, and what they think of the pink tower looming 85 feet over the rest of the strip mall — what they think of Casa Bonita.

I pocket a hand sanitizer and get out of my car. Approaching the building — which is connected, absurdly, to an arts and crafts shop and to an Adventure Dental — the sense of desolation I'd been anticipating rises. The fountain outside the front entrance, which I remember as being extravagant, blooming, is static and empty, save for a few patches of ice frozen along the tile. I step underneath the front arch and a familiar sign comes into view:

> Because we feature LIVE ENTERTAINMENT & because there is NO COVER CHARGE we must require every person over 2yrs of age to purchase a dinner before entering the RESTAURANT. *We believe that you will understand after entering.*

The words *FUCK 12* are scrawled in sharpie over the text. Two

FedEx shipping notices have been attached to the front door, as well as an envelope addressed to Robert Wheaton, the owner of Casa's Bonita's parent company, Star Buffet. Taped to a window is a note from management: *Casa Bonita is closed due to Colorado-mandated regulations during the COVID-19 pandemic. We plan to reopen when permitted to do so.*

Most Colorado businesses opened their doors by the end of May, but "[Casa Bonita] remains shuttered," *Denver Westword* reported back in early September. "Star Buffet, the mysterious parent company of Casa Bonita, is not taking calls . . . considering that the kitschy theme park of a restaurant, the forerunner of the eatertainment experience, can seat more people than some sports stadiums, staying closed until there's a COVID-19 vaccine might make sense. Still, the current silence seems almost as weird as Casa Bonita itself."

Casa Bonita's troubles were foreshadowed early in the pandemic, with *The Denver Post* reporting that employees' mid-March paychecks bounced "days after they were deposited," and that some "were even charged by their banks for those last deposits, which were returned for lack of sufficient funds. *The Denver Post* has reached out to Star Buffet's CEO Robert Wheaton and the corporate office multiple times over phone and email for comment but has not heard back."

Standing out in the cold, it strikes me that *Westword* is right: Robert Wheaton and Star Buffet's silence really does seem as weird as Casa Bonita itself, and, given the apparent treatment of their employees, perhaps even sinister. And maybe it's the boredom or the isolation or the sense that life's been stuck in stasis for nearly a year now, but the mystery of it all feels so much like a blast of serotonin that I almost don't recognize it at first.

Something's up at Casa Bonita: I want to figure out why no one's heard from Star Buffet, if they plan to reopen, if they ever paid their employees. And I suspect that, if I could just get in touch with him, Robert Wheaton has the answers.

Casa Bonita as Object of Sincere and Ironic Appreciation
In a 2003 episode of *South Park* titled "Casa Bonita," Cartman about sums it up: "Casa Bonita is my most favorite place in the world," he explains, breathlessly. "It's a big Mexican restaurant, where they have, like, cliff jumpers, and a haunted cave, and all kinds of stuff."

The last of five novelty restaurants originally branded under the "Casa Bonita" moniker, the Colorado location opened in 1974 and is oft-cited by the likes of *Atlas Obscura* as one of the Denver area's premier oddities. Built on the site of a former tuberculosis sanitarium, Casa Bonita is a completely indoor, 52,000-square-foot restaurant and theme park that can seat over 1,000 guests at a time. When visitors first enter, they're greeted by a byzantine queue line, modeled after a cave system, which at once resembles that of an elaborate amusement park attraction and of a high school cafeteria. Inching through the line, customers place their order, receive their meals on a lunch tray, and, after paying, are led out of the cavern and into a lush, dimly-lit dining area that's designed to invoke a tropical rainforest as well as an undoubtedly problematic conception of a "Mexican" village. So massive in scope that certain sections are a full quarter-mile from the kitchen, Casa Bonita's interior is extravagant. String-lights hang from the ceiling, fake palm trees branch out of corridors, and themed areas bleed seamlessly into one another — "haunted" caverns, painted storefronts, an old-timey gift shop, a magician's theater, and, in an obvious conceptual outlier, a '90s-style arcade. During operating hours, the paths are replete with actors dressed as explorers, pirates, gorillas, and outlaws, various combinations of whom perform near-constant skits in the glow of a spotlight from atop Casa Bonita's centerpiece: a majestic, artificial waterfall surrounded by a thirty-foot cliffside that spills out into an idyllic (if fenced off) tropical lagoon.

I can imagine what you're thinking: that Casa Bonita is absurd and kitschy and vulgar; that it represents a delirious commitment to late capitalism; that it sounds a little as if someone decided to start selling Chile Rellenos at a B-grade Pirates of the Caribbean knockoff. And it is those things. But when you step out of the queue and into the dining area and the lights dim and the waterfall first comes into view—there is, genuinely, a feeling of almost romantic disorientation. It's difficult to square that you are, in the same moment, standing in the middle of a strip-mall off Colfax Avenue, and looking out across the expanse of a fully realized artificial rainforest.

And you know what? It's a marvel. It's fucking beautiful.

Undermining the technical achievement of its aesthetic beauty, of course, is the inherent racism of the restaurant's design. Despite billing itself as "Mexican-themed," the restaurant doesn't invoke Mexico so much as it does a broad amalgamation of Central and South America as it existed—and, in many cases, continues to exist—in the American consciousness. That the restaurant is modeled after a region that has faced a violent history of colonialism feels almost too on-the-nose to begin unpacking. It's not subtle, presenting the various regions as a lawless tropical paradise brimming with mystery and ripe for exploration by a predominantly white audience. Indeed, much of Casa Bonita's visual flavor is rooted in a kind of old-school, *Heart of Darkness* style racism. It's Rainforest Café by way of a Speedy Gonzalez cartoon.

The last time I visited, back in June of 2019, I came with my then-girlfriend and some of her visiting family. It was only a few weeks before we ended things, and I remember the spark of awe and confusion in her cousins' eyes as they first entered the building, and how absurd I felt to be wistfully sipping a margarita as I stared across the waterfall with my forearm against a guardrail. I spent so much of that afternoon on my phone, and suffering through our mandatory enchiladas and taco salads, we watched as a hunter chased a gorilla through our section, nearly knocking over a waitress who'd been precariously balancing a tray of drinks on her arm.

There's a delirium to that image that I suspect will stay with me for some time, and shortly after visiting the strip mall, I reach out to ask old friends if they'd be willing to share their experiences at Casa Bonita. I want to make sure that I'm not mythologizing the place too much, for one thing, that I'm not making it out to be something that it isn't. Besides, the holiday season has made my apartment lonelier than ever, and it's as good an excuse as any to hop on a Zoom call with some folks, many of whom I haven't seen in person for nearly a year now.

Almost everyone I speak to has a story: one friend tells me about an aborted attempt to hit up Casa Bonita on prom night; another remembers their aunt getting hammered and blasting away well-dressed terrorists in *Time Crisis*; a third recalls a middle-school field trip that ended with an acquaintance clutching an unflattering caricature and weeping on the bus ride home. Others reminisce lyrically about the wishing well, Black Bart's Cavern, the fire juggling, and the endless sopapilla refills that could be summoned by simply raising a small flag mounted to each table.

"It's kind of like Disneyland," one friend tells me. "You know that there's underlying work that you're not seeing, but they still find a way to make it a magical experience."

That reaction is not at all uncommon. Despite it all—the long lines, the derided cuisine, the gummy surfaces, and the ignorant depiction of Mexico—Casa Bonita remains beloved in the metro-area. It's not just a cult favorite, either: the establishment was named the 2016 Public Health Champion by Jefferson County for its exemplary commitment to food safety, and in March of 2015, it was even christened a historical landmark by the city of Lakewood Historical Society.

"Lakewood is ahead of the curve in valuing this place as a formal landmark," Denver-based architectural historian Poppie Gullet tells me. "Regardless of what you think of the kitsch or dubious authenticity, the restaurant is one of a kind . . . the elaborate pink stucco tower, the absurdly engineered interior, and the long-running [performances] show us the importance of tradition at Casa Bonita, even if that tradition is indoor cliff-diving and sub-par sopapillas."

That sense of tradition—that we've grown up with it, that it's been around forever, that it's part of what makes Denver, *Denver*—likely has something to do with Coloradoans' fascination with the restaurant. For many of us, Casa Bonita is a space that holds meaning in no small part because of the ways that meaning has shifted over time. Most of us are first introduced to the place as kids, when, in the words of one friend, "you can't even really appreciate what's so special about it," only to return years later as an adult, when all of a sudden, "you notice the cracks in the wall," and can even consume alcohol while you gawk at the absurdity. The disconnect between these two experiences is staggering, and it speaks to much of Casa Bonita's charm.

"Every time I go it feels bigger," another friend tells me, "which is crazy, because usually, places like that have more mystery when you're younger. Casa Bonita is the opposite, though. As an adult, I'm dumbfounded."

A telling trend appears across these conversations: nearly everyone I speak to seems to think that the general public's appreciation for Casa Bonita is rooted in irony, while nonetheless describing their own affection as wholly sincere. The expectation betrays a kind of embarrassment. What does it mean to adore Casa Bonita? How can one reconcile a space that is at once unique and strange and brimming with painstakingly detailed life, but that nonetheless represents both a monument to our colonialist history and a crass appeal to consumerism?

In some ways, it's the problem of growing up anywhere in the United States: so many of us still have affection for it, even as we know that we probably shouldn't.

Casa Bonita as Basic HTML Web Page

The eccentricities of Casa Bonita's business model—the dinner-dependent entrance fee, the expansive interior, the astronomical operating costs—presumably help to explain its failure to succeed as a franchise, the difficulty in reopening at a limited capacity, and, of course, the final round of bounced paychecks back in March. Over the years, Star Buffet has been in and out of bankruptcy, and the other four Casa Bonita locations shut down without much fanfare: Fort Worth's in 1985, Little Rock and Oklahoma City's in 1993, and Tulsa's in 2005, although it briefly reopened in 2008 before a massive snowstorm closed business for good in 2011. It makes sense that Casa Bonita is struggling in wake of the shutdown; what doesn't make sense is Star Buffet's silence.

I do some digging.

Casa Bonita's official website went down back in April, but Star Buffet's still comes up when you type it into Google. Holed up like always on the futon in my apartment, I open starbuffet.com on my laptop. The last vestiges of natural light are disappearing through my window, and a bright red triangle with an exclamation mark in the center appears on my screen. Underneath are the words: *YOUR CONNECTION IS NOT PRIVATE.* A note at the bottom of the page warns that the website's security certificate expired on August 24: *Proceed to starbuffet.com (unsafe).*

I glance to either side of me, as though there is anyone around to question my judgement, and I continue past the notice to a barren HTML webpage that would have looked outdated even in the early 2000s'. Star Buffet's logo is displayed in the top right corner—a gold star with a black plastic fork on one side and a knife on the other—and below are the words, *Welcome to StarBuffet. com. For a Store Listing click here. Investor Information click here.* It's unbelievably sketchy, and honestly, the layout is so half-assed that I can't help but wonder if the whole enterprise isn't a front for something more suspect. The gulf between Casa Bonita's attention to detail and its parent company's lax professionalism is glaring.

Suddenly, Star Buffet seems very much the kind of operation that would stiff its workers in the middle of a global pandemic.

Store Listing brings me to a minimalist catalog of twenty additional restaurants and properties owned by Star Buffet, over half of which appear to be entries in a Midwest chain called JB's Restaurant. I take a screenshot of the listing, resolve to return to it later if I can't find another way to get in touch with the company.

Poking around _Investor Information_, I discover a PDF of an old press release with Robert Wheaton's phone number at the bottom. For a moment, I think that perhaps I've found a way to access him that other Denver journalists have somehow missed, and I let my hopes rise as I dial the number.

It rings once, and then a voice on the other side of the line says, "The number you are trying to reach is not in service."

Casa Bonita as Creative Community

"Yeah, I've been trying to figure it out too," Stephanie Simon, a former Casa Bonita entertainer tells me over a Zoom call. It's November 23rd, I'm a few days into a listless fall break away from classes and teaching and predetermined interactions with anyone at all. Stephanie and I met over Facebook, where I'd found her and a few other former employees by typing _Casa Bonita_ into the search bar and filtering users by their work histories, figuring that if there was no way to get in touch with Star Buffet directly, that I may as well start with its workers. "I've never met Wheaton myself," Stephanie continues. "I know he came in a couple of times while I was working there, but no, I don't know what's going on with Star Buffet."

Stephanie has green hair, sleeves inked across her forearms. She's a tattoo artist now, but between 2008 and 2011 she worked as a server, entertainer, and manager at Casa Bonita. "I'd never been there before applying," she explains. "But I'm a sucker for kitschy places like that. I got offered a job at Six Flags as a caricature artist around that time, too, but I ended up taking the job at Casa Bonita because . . . " she trails off, shrugs. "It's beautiful. It really is. It's so unique and it has so much history and I wanted to be a part of it."

"You're constantly acting," she explains. "Every 15 minutes there's another show that you're performing in. There are a few different sketches — the gorilla skit, the gunfight — but you're putting on essentially the same ten-minute show over and over again. I'd get pushed into the water from the cliff, then swim underneath the waterfall, go back up the stairs, dry off as fast as I could, and then we'd start the next show."

Former stuntman and entertainment director, Corey Rhodes, doesn't have much information about Star Buffet, either, but he shares Stephanie's enthusiasm for his time there. He's eager to talk about the place, and his eyes light up as he lists off his favorite performances. "We also had a pirate show," he continues, beaming, "which was one of my favorites because it had a sweet, choreographed sword fight." Corey developed an interest in acting through high school theater and applied to Casa Bonita just before graduation. He's thirty-four now, finishing up his degree in film and television at CU Denver. "Working there was my first extensive foray into performing," he tells me, "doing fifteen shows a night for all those years."

As entertainment director, Corey made it his mission to promote improvisation among the staff. He even found ways to keep the twice-per-hour puppet shows interesting, reimagining workplace shenanigans — like, for instance, the actor in the gorilla costume repeatedly sneaking up on the cotton candy vendor — into fodder for the scripts. "The kids had no idea [these shows] were written about the restaurant, of course," Corey tells me. "They just thought it was funny that the puppet was throwing up cotton candy."

Other Casa Bonita higher-ups, too, began to promote a culture of creative collaboration. "We had a manager who would have us come in every Saturday and do an improv class," Stephanie tells me. "We'd get a box of donuts, go into the theater and just run exercises with each other. It really gave me a lot of creative skill sets."

That feeling of positivity extended to the clientele, at least during server Kristina Moonie's tenure. "People definitely didn't come there for the food," she tells me, "but there weren't many negative experiences of people *complaining* about the food, either. Everyone knows what they're in for, and the atmosphere is just so inviting. My sister was a diver at the time, and she would make it a point to bring [costumed performers] over to my tables during our shifts together, so kids would get to be served by a princess or whatever. It's tough to be in a bad mood there."

Kristina's sister, Michelle Moonie, first auditioned to be a diver and performer without ever having dived or acted a day in her life. "I was originally just auditioning to get pictures of me jumping off the cliff to impress my friends," she says. "I never actually planned on working there, but even in auditioning, the people were so fun to work with that I was drawn to the place. One thing led to another and I stayed on for about four years, and after that, I actually ended up doing another diving show on the East Coast for a while."

Michelle describes herself as having "a much more normal job now," working as an assistant to a financial adviser in Santa Fe. "It was unexpected," she says. "All through high school, I was the one not getting parts in plays. I didn't have any acting abilities. But at Casa Bonita, the diver plays the gorilla, the pirate—the diver does everything. By the end of my time there I was great at performing in front of hundreds of people. That place was my life. It was chaos, but I loved it."

Casa Bonita as Chaotic Outgrowth of Late-Stage Capitalism

"I could write a book about that place," Michelle Moonie tells me, when, after realizing that she knows as much about Star Buffet as I do, I decide to indulge myself and ask for the wildest stories that she can remember from her time there. "All the chaos, all the performances that went bad, all the people getting hurt mid-show. People would fall in the water unexpectedly, or we'd be juggling fire and I'd drop a club off stage . . . it was kind of horrifying. The fire marshal shut down the juggling shortly after I left."

Michelle tells me that once, during the gorilla show, a worker struck her head on a rock after getting caught in some guide ropes, eventually leaving mid-show with a concussion. "We skipped most of our lines and jumped to the end," Michelle says, "so that I could get pushed into the water and check on her." This commitment to staying in character was something of a company-wide directive: "As long as there's an audience, you don't break character no matter what happens." It's an edict that weighs the preservation of Casa Bonita's fictive dream above worker safety, and the attempted implication is clear: *no one gets hurt here; this show won't stop for anything.*

Michelle goes on to tell me about a particularly excruciating set of shows performed for a single audience member. "She was the first customer of the day, just sitting alone by herself on a lunch break or something. It was painful."

Across each interview, it becomes clear that, for as chaotic a setting as Casa Bonita could be, the guests themselves were responsible for a great deal of its unpredictability. "Every once in a while, a drunk thirty-something guy would try to fight the gorilla," Stephanie Simon explains. "One time we had a guy come in dressed as a banana trying to distract the gorilla, but you can use that to your advantage as a performer."

Even more common were guests trying to jump into the lagoon. "I'd hear a splash and think, *oh jeez, I don't think anyone's performing right now,*" says Corey Rhodes. "And I'd run down to the pool as [the jumper] was climbing out, and I'd try to cut them off as they ran away."

Jumpers were most common on Friday and Saturday nights, when softball players from the Lakewood recreation league would have a few too many undersized Fat Tires, or when thirty-somethings spread across the metro-area would reunite for a raucous nostalgia hit. The issue was so prevalent that it resulted in Casa Bonita eventually hiring security guards.

"The jumpers would be banned for life. They'd get their pictures taken and get fined," Michelle explains. "A few of them had a good getaway plan. They knew the route through the restaurant to get out the door quickly, and they'd have a getaway driver ready outside."

Nostalgic daredevils weren't the only thing that the staff had to be prepared for. "We had a rule that if the actor in the gorilla suit ever fell in the pool, that it was on the head of everyone working," Stephanie continues. "It was a heavy costume and the water was deep."

When I ask her about this, Michelle sort of sighs, exasperated but affectionate, the way you might look back on the quirks of an old friend or partner that you've long since stepped away from. She explains that no one in the gorilla costume fell in during her time there, but that there are rumors that the policy was inspired by an incident from the late '70s. "All-hands-on-deck," Michelle says. "If the mariachi band are the ones closest to the pool, then they're absolutely expected to dive in and save the gorilla."

I'll confess that the absurdity of the image—a dozen or so people, many dressed as pirates and outlaws and Indiana Jones types, all jumping into the pool at once to pull out a guy in a gorilla suit—struck me at first as being deeply funny. Like so many things, though, the intensity of the presentation obscures the reality. "You had the real potential of someone drowning," Stephanie tells me.

Kristina, the former server, echoes this sentiment. "We didn't get a lot of training specifically around rescuing the gorilla."

Although it doesn't usually manifest in such a life-threatening manner, the potential OSHA violations described here are very much on-brand with the rest of Casa Bonita's surreal aura. "Weird things were always happening," Stephanie tells me. "At some point, MTV had interest in setting a reality show there, and *Ghost Hunters* had their eyes on us for a while." I perk up at that, and she's quick to clarify that Casa Bonita is, to her knowledge, not even remotely haunted, though there are stories floating around, she says, "Like, *oh, there's a diver that haunts the pool*. That kind of thing."

The stories are endless: sopapilla flags raising of their own accord, cliffside proposals, underground burlesque shows, secret concerts, an album release party for The Fray's second record, rowdy *Book of Mormon* after-parties, appearances by Joseph Gordon-Levitt, improv calamities, belligerent customers.

It's a pandora's box of wild stories. It's an almost unfathomable amount of possibility.

Casa Bonita as Mystery Box

It's Wednesday, November 25th, and, alone in my apartment, I can tell that I'm in an up-period of isolation because sticky notes are scattered across my desk, and I've written and circled, *CASA BONITA* in the direct center of my white-board. Word clouds branching off it read, *GHOSTS, ROBERT WHEATON, STAR BUFFET, CASA BONITA AS UNDERRATED CREATIVE EPICENTER*, and *THE FRAY*. I feel a little like the protagonist in a David Fincher movie, just a step or two away from pinning newspaper articles to my corkboard.

I'm not at all discouraged by my abject failure to discern any useful information regarding Star Buffet, Robert Wheaton, or the circumstances surrounding Casa Bonita employees' final, mid-March paycheck. If anything, a peek behind the curtain has only made me more resolute in my conviction that the deeper I dig, the more there will be to uncover. I'm feeling excited for the first time in ages, and I decide that it's finally time to cold-call Star Buffet's other assets in hopes of finding someone who could get me in touch with Robert Wheaton.

I pull up the list of Star Buffet's properties: the first is a JB's Restaurant in Rexburg, Idaho. I dial the number, and it doesn't even ring; instead, a robotic voice informs me that *the subscriber you have dialed is not in service.*

I try the next property, a Buddy Freddy's in Plant City, Florida. Then a JB's in Miles City, Montana. Another in Jonesboro, Arkansas. Havre, Montana. Dalhart, Texas.

The results are always the same: *the number you have dialed is not in service.* Sometimes the phone just keeps ringing.

At last, someone picks up at a restaurant in Montana. "Hello," the person on the other end of the line answers, and I quickly embellish my credentials. "I can't give you Robert's number," the voice says. "But I can give you Steve's. He's the vice president." I thank him and transcribe the digits.

Steve's area code covers the entire state of Montana, and I'm surprised when he picks up on the second ring. "Steve here," he says, gruff, unassuming, and I breathlessly repeat my backstory. "I'm trying to figure out what's up at Casa Bonita," I say. "Can you tell me anything about what's happening over there? Do you know if those workers ever got paid?"

"I only handle the family restaurants," Steve tells me. "Casa Bonita is Robert's baby. You'll have to ask him." He recites his boss's number, and it's only after I've written it down that he seems to second guess himself. "Hey wait a sec," he says. "How'd you get this number."

I don't want to get anyone in trouble. "A very, very deep Google search," I tell him.

Right away I call Robert, and as the phone rings, it occurs to me that maybe I should have slowed down a bit: this is a big moment, and I have no idea who I'm dealing with here. My heart beats in a way that it hasn't in months, and I wonder, somewhat inexplicably, if this is a bad idea, if there are nefarious reasons he's stayed so far off the grid for as long as he has. I consider what I'll say when he answers, resolve to withhold my last name.

Wheaton's phone rings four times, five, six, before clicking over to a voicemail message. *You've reached Robert Wheaton,* says a woman's voice. *Please leave a message after the beep, or email Robert at . . .*

Always one step ahead, I think.

I draft an email: *Hi there, Robert – my name is Chris, and I got your number from Steve. I'm working on a profile piece about Casa Bonita, and I had a few questions about the shut-down and about its future. I'm wondering if you might be available to comment?*

I read over the draft, and just as the thought crosses my mind that this mystery maybe isn't as seismic as I've made it out to be, I get a text message from a friend: *For your research,* says Riley. I click the link she's forwarded, and it pulls up a *Denver Channel* article dated November 17th, titled, "No, Casa Bonita isn't permanently closed, but it's not likely to reopen anytime soon, owners say."

Christ, I think. *They scooped me.*

I scan the article for Wheaton's comment. It's short and to the point: "Our plan is to open the business as soon as we believe it's legally possible," he says. "My feeling is the guidelines [around maximum capacity for indoor dining] will not change until there is a [widely available] vaccine. Casa Bonita has been around 50 years and we're hopeful that it's going to be around for another 50 years."

He's got nothing to say about the displaced workers, nothing about the bounced checks. Just as its performers were required to stay in character even in the event of injury, the conservation of Casa Bonita – of its illusions, of its legacy, of what it means to those of us here in Denver – is half the point, its perpetuation an end in itself.

Casa Bonita as Grim Reality

When asked about his hopes for Casa Bonita, former entertainment director Corey Rhodes thought for a moment, shook his head, smiled. "Man, working there was important to who I am as a person," he had told me. "Some of the craziest, wackiest times that I've ever had were at that place. I just hope it's around for a long time."

"I wish I had enough to buy it," former entertainer and manager Stephanie Simon had told me. "It would be so devastating to lose such a weird and special part of Colorado. Do you know how many Easter eggs are hidden throughout that place? There's this section in the haunted mine that has all these stalactites and stalagmites, and people carve their names into the texture. It's like Meow Wolf or something, just a gigantic piece of interactive artwork."

"We tear enough shit down in Denver to put up crappy luxury apartments and storage garages," she'd said. "This is a piece of history."

Michelle Moonie, the former diver, had expressed a similar sentiment. "A lot of people out here in Santa Fe haven't heard of it, so it's kind of crazy to try to explain to them that I was a diver in a restaurant. It's such a big part of my life — it's tough to lose that. I had been hoping that one day I could bring my kids there."

Michelle had proceeded to tell me about a friend who'd been working at Casa Bonita in March when COVID-19 first began to ripple across the country. "She had worked there for ten years, and now she's working at a bank," Michelle said. "Which is . . . pretty different. Everybody had to move on. For a while they were all waiting for the call, but then, one by one they realized it wasn't coming anytime soon."

There are some, of course, who have no interest in coming back following their treatment by Star Buffet. "At this point, I don't see myself returning," former employee Felicity Akers told *The Denver Post* back in April, after her paycheck bounced. "It's hard to go back to a place that doesn't respect you enough to pay you for the work that you've done."

"Casa Bonita will always have a place in my heart," Felicity wrote in a public, widely shared Facebook status on March 29. "To all of the upper management: thank you for trusting me and teaching me to be successful in everything that I did. To all of the friends I've made: thank you for being there for me on some of my worst and best days . . . To Bob Wheaton and the corporate office: I hope you fully understand the pain you have put many families through that live paycheck to paycheck, and [who] are now struggling because they are missing three weeks of pay . . . almost every employee has been around for years, not because corporate or the owner treated them well, [but] because we are a family, and we love working at a place that brings so many people happiness. None of us are happy today. We are all angry."

I feel ashamed for having been excited about any of this.

Felicity's testimony is indicative of a larger pattern of exploitation on the part of Star Buffet, from the bounced paychecks to the negligent safety procedures to the clear prioritization of the facility's simulacrum. That former employees hold near-universal affection for Casa Bonita makes its parent company's negligence all the more duplicitous, but to argue that Star Buffett is unique in its exploitation would be a failure of imagination.

In many ways, Star Buffet's treatment of its workforce models the kind of economic violence, even colonialism, so dreamily masked in its tropical interiors.

This is what we do.

From Amazon quietly withdrawing hazard pay to Disney laying off 100,000 theme-park workers to save less than 20% of the last *Avengers* movie's total gross, this year has made more visible than ever what has always been true: that most conveniences are made possible only by the exploitation of labor; that our most essential workers are often considered the most expendable; that our iPhones are produced in Uyghur concentration camps; and that any luxury is just that, an illusion that we're willing to pretend is not illusory.

The specifics of Casa Bonita's story are sensational—the

building is phantasmagorical, of course, and Star Buffet's elusiveness is intriguingly enigmatic — but there was never anything special about this story, never any mystery. Just another barred-off restaurant. Just another workforce screwed over by a corporation. Just another beautiful thing crushed by a virus that has spread along trade routes and flight paths, by our federal government's utter disregard for its populace, by America's delusional insistence that the show must go on.

Casa Bonita as Potentially Misplaced Symbol of Hope

It's Thursday, November 26th, Thanksgiving, and once more I pull into the lot off Colfax.

My day has been, of course, uneventful — a Zoom call with my parents, another with my sister, and a third planned with friends for the evening. Almost everything's closed, and there are only a few cars in the lot, just a pedestrian or two at the crosswalk. It all looks so much like how I imagine the world these days.

Once again, I've returned with my mask and my hand sanitizer, even though the mystery is solved, mostly, even though there was never really any mystery to begin with.

"I heard through the grapevine that the general manager and the assistant G.M. go in every day or so to maintain [Case Bonita]," Stephanie Simon had told me. "They care about the place. They're passionate about it. They want it to be ready to go when this is over."

As I step out of my car and onto the pavement, I'm thinking of the Fed Ex notices taped to the door from my last visit, but still, I want it to be true — that these managers come by every day or so, of their own accord, to help keep Casa Bonita afloat. There's something romantic about it, something beautiful. Whether owing to an inherent optimism, or the simple accident of having been born here, I still want to believe in this place, and I've returned here with a letter of my own.

To whom it may concern, I've written. *I'm working on a story about Casa Bonita, and I heard that you come by a few times a week to maintain the dining area. I think that's lovely and I'd like to talk to you about it. If you're interested, you can reach me at —*

I don't linger to stare into the empty fountain, or to admire the signs and graffiti, or to wallow in the sense that I am staring at a dead thing. I tape the envelope to the door beside a Fed-Ex slip, turn around, and put my hands in my pockets as I pace back to my car.

"God, I just love Casa Bonita," my friend Lauren Lipp-Newman told me at the start of this project, her voice crackling over an unstable internet connection. It was the first time we'd seen each other since before the pandemic, and at first, I almost didn't recognize her. "You've made me want to go back so bad, talking about it like this," she'd said, and she laughed in a way that's become so familiar throughout this year — resigned, a little manic. It's wasn't a real laugh, more like she couldn't believe any of it: the pandemic, the dead-on-arrival response, the devastation, the death, the human cost of it all, the unbelievable feeling of stasis, like where we are now is where we'll always be, like we're all out of stories. "Nothing sounds better," she'd said, "when you're locked down, and stuck at home, than standing in line for an hour to watch a bunch of kitschy bullshit."

"It's the opposite of quarantine," she'd said.

After getting back into my car, I turn on the ignition, queue up a song by Modern Baseball. I keep meaning to shift out of park, but I don't; I just sit there. The thought crosses my mind that if I wait long enough I might encounter the kind of miracle you'd see in a holiday special: the G.M. pulling up at the last possible second before I leave, and I imagine them getting out of their car, taking their keys out of their pocket, and sighing to themselves as they approach the iconic pink tower to complete an act of service for this ridiculous fucking place that feels so much like America.

I have nowhere to be, and so I crank up the volume, nod along to the lyrics.

And I know that waiting here on Thanksgiving should feel bleak, lonely, but honestly, it feels an awful lot like hope. Hope that the managers will show up. Hope that the pandemic will end. Hope that Casa Bonita will reopen. That someone else will buy the place. That the employees let go at the start of quarantine received their back pay. That the employees who held out for as long as they could, who are spread out now across banks and breweries and grocery stores, that they'll be able to come back if they still want to. That this isn't all for nothing. That wearing a mask matters. That social distancing matters. That phone banking matters, and voter registration drives, and canvassing. That mutual aid matters, and staying in the streets. That art will still be here. That our communities will be waiting for us. That I will not spend next Thanksgiving alone. That even after everything, this country is worth hoping for. That what comes next will be better. That the world we return to will be one where strange and absurd spaces not only still exist, but that we can feel secure inside of them, confident that we are not risking our own lives or the lives of strangers, and that our choice to patronize these spaces is ethical and sound. That all of us will make it. That on the other side of this thing, we can hold up our glasses and laugh as an actor in a gorilla costume barrels past our table. That the sopapillas will always be unlimited. That we can tip the shit out of the server who just walked them a quarter-mile to our table. That we take in every second of the mystery. That we'll recognize all of this for what it is: precious and absurd and impermanent. That we'll smile like we mean it. Jesus Christ. God willing. Holy shit.

BILL CHRISTOPHERSEN

THANKSGIVING DAY

Forget the louring inflatables,
the flotilla of floats, the disciplined
hoopla of marching bands. In Central Park,
fall's ghetto flamboyance steals the show.
The concentrated wrack, the brilliant litter
of spent vegetable matter; the lake's quicksilver;
the ducks in V formation like a Bronx
street gang . . . Say what? Here's a flying squad
of motorcycle cops, counterpointing
downdrafts of leaves, the ducks' choreographed
moonwalking . . . Thanks be to lucent pigments,
bleeding xanthophylls, carotenoids;
dried leaves curled to a fare-thee-well —
the maximalist poetry of dying.

DEBORAH ALLBRITAIN

FROM THE KITCHEN IN MARCH

The downward slope
is calling. Even if
you ride it out

there is no even keeling, no
seamless, just
an ozone of what-have-yous,
a bread and butter
demeanor.

There's no burn
here, only a lemon votive,

a grocery store
bouquet
of drooped mums.

Not the life
you had in mind which
even if you'd had
you'd say instead,
this please.

There is no
zinnia milk or a way
to pajama dreary and
sleep it away.

Do get over yourself, Cupcake.
The outweighs are drops
of cream in your

Darjeeling, steamed water
from the old tap reheated

and reheated, lemon, honey,
given just like that.

DAY AFTER VALENTINE'S

Expectation
is a genetic headache from Neanderthals.

Take mediocrity in its simplest form,
bring it in from the garage, fill its stark
nothing with stark nothing.

Take calamity, toss the broken porcelain
in the sink, it's only earth-living.

The middle height of middling does not
overextend or dash, does not pretend to be
desire seldom seen in public.

It will not say it loves you or pull something
cashmere down your shoulders. Instead,

red camisoles speak middling, no less awful
than your dark mouth in the distance

that swims in the blood of so-so.
It's simple wisdom really. Endure.

Even a cherrystone clam
provides some small delicious.

MY DAUGHTER TEXTS A PICTURE AND CALLS IT REHAB BRAIDS

Today I read Jane Kenyon's poem about peonies.
How they loll and luxuriate, not quite decent.
But what of my shaken flower asleep in the detox wing
somewhere in Laguna Beach. I cannot prop her up
with stakes and twine, can't lift her face sunward
or square the law of averages that no blooms shall topple.
What is it going to take, all this mulch and wait.
Fuck Jane's peonies. Behind the garage where
nothing grows and no sprinklers reach, my little flock
of agapanthus, my trash flowers, look how you muscle
through every winter, souls resting in your amethyst heads,
all those stars with summer inside them. Walk with me.

It would stay in the air forever, eventually
flying off and spinning into the horizon.

A NEW REVENUE STREAM

It wasn't strictly legal.

Jeremy Neck was using The Whirl Corporation's official font on a sign he'd made for his new business.

Because even if throwing items off the Sutherland-Dowd Bridge seemed fun, people in cars would never stop if they knew he was Unaffiliated. But, with the stolen font, people could safely assume that his business was part of the massive and growing Whirl Corporation — which was getting terrifically close to having Absolute Ownership of all businesses and services.

The Desjardins family pulled over to Jeremy's Scenic View Area. They picked the dresser with the porcelain knobs. 17 Credits seemed reasonable — a small price to pay for an exciting/new/family activity.

DesjardinsDad said to DesjardinsMom and the two DesjardinsKids, "All right, DesjardinsGang. Let's give this thing the old heave-ho on three."

"One! Two! Three!" DesjardinsFamily said, and the family threw the dresser over the side of the bridge. The parents quickly lifted up their two little guys so they could see the dresser hit the shallow water and splinter on the rocks. They all laughed/laughed/laughed. DesjardinsDad patted Jeremy on the back.

Jeremy Neck was producing fun for anyone who stopped, and he tossed a smile to each and every customer. It turned out that Jeremy was very good at increasing the Happiness Level of strangers.

And, Jeremy figured, once the Whirl Corporation saw how successfully he could develop a New Revenue Stream, they wouldn't care how it got started or who was using whose fonts. They were always sniffing out new Developments. Sure he was messing with Economic Compliance Laws now, but they'd eventually be thrilled that such a wonderful and imaginative person had gotten their attention.

Jeremy knew that the Whirl Corporation CFO famously had "The ends justify the means" tattooed across his face.

This new business of throwing items off the bridge could be like an audition/interview. He'd generate some Economic Prosperity to show Whirl what he could do. And they would Accumulate him and his business into the Whirl Corporation family. And his life would finally perk up. Accumulation meant a corporate job and a future. It was a steady paycheck, free breakfast on Fridays, dating ambitious women, Economic Prosperity.

Economic Compliance Laws couldn't matter when the Credits were coming in this easily. A great business idea was a great business idea.

It had all popped into his head naturally enough. Two days ago, he'd been making the 4-hour drive home after another failed interview up north at one of The Whirl Corporation Executive Branches when he came to the Sutherland-Dowd Bridge. It was so plain and old-seeming. There weren't any advertisement GIFs on the bridge, and it wasn't even divided into bumpy and smooth lanes for Basic and Elite Toll Packages.

He'd pulled his ancient little pickup truck over to the ScenicView Area and looked over the side. 100 feet down were rocks and sand and a very shallow river that was dried to almost nothing from the August heat. And he got the impulse to throw something off the bridge. It popped into his head — just like any other idea would — like what to buy or what to watch.

He felt his body get warm with the rush of pre-purchase as he pulled up his Available Credit Transfer App on his phone.

Except there wasn't a person or a machine to transfer Available

Credits to. It wasn't right. There was always a person or a machine to transfer Credits to. But not here. Throwing something off the Sutherland-Dowd Bridge would cost nothing.

And Jeremy looked around/around/around to make darn sure. But it was just him up there.

In the back of his pickup, he had a small, upholstered chair that his Nana had poop-ruined.

And despite the bubbling wrong-feeling, and his guilty, left/right/left/right looks, he launched the chair toward a gaggle of rocks down below. For free.

It splintered and destroyed the morning silence with a loud and shaking crack. It made Jeremy Neck feel like he was full of blood and power and chest muscles. He wasn't a Junior Executive yet, but it was a very Junior Executive feeling.

Jeremy thought that if he felt this good from throwing something off the bridge, maybe other people would too. Maybe people would even transfer Credits for it. And The Whirl Corporation would offer him a high-level position. Maybe with the Division of Revenue Stream Development or the Prosperity Acquisition Department. It didn't matter. He was flexible.

Destroying something that wasn't quite broken/garbage just felt right.

And this feeling made Jeremy hop back into his truck and make a beeline for the closest Whirl Army Thrift Store. He needed stuff to sell that wasn't quite broken/garbage.

Jeremy found the owner of the Sutherland-Dowd Bridge. He was an older man who wanted to be called by his old Army nickname — Nails. And Nails was currently being sued by Whirl for Non-Compliance, because he refused to sell the bridge for the price they offered. The case was going to a very pro-Whirl court, and it was only a matter of time. Nails coughed a lot, and while Nails thought it over, Jeremy pretended to cough a couple of times.

Nails said, "Shit — I need Availables no matter where they're coming from." So he agreed to the 20% that Jeremy offered.

And now, two days later, Jeremy's business was in full swing. As soon as the DesjardinsFamily left, others were ready. Cars stopped, curious people threw something over, laughed/laughed/laughed, and got back into their cars, feeling a little lighter.

The business was developing and growing—which was the first step of his plan.

But at one point, when a couple looked over the edge to watch their glass-top coffee table smash, their faces didn't glow. The corners of their mouths dropped, and their shoulders sagged.

"Hmm," the man said. "There's just already so much garbage down there."

"Hmm," the woman said.

"Hmm," Jeremy agreed.

So, Jeremy posted to the WhirlTempsAreHappy app, and within seconds, he got messages. Twelve minutes later, there were two very old women who said they didn't have actual names. They were very ready to pick up garbage. They were desperate and had very low Happiness Levels. One got nosebleeds a lot, but she said it wouldn't interfere.

Jeremy certainly implied that he worked for Whirl.

There became a clean rhythm to Jeremy's new Revenue Stream. Jeremy transferred Credits from customers, gave them their smashable merchandise, and smiled/smiled/smiled.

And the nameless women picked up the broken pieces under the bridge—cutting the bigger ones with a handsaw or smashing them with a hammer—and tossed the pieces into the rented dumpster off to the side. Nails even helped clean up—partly because he'd always loved his beautiful property and partly because he wanted a shot at the nameless women, especially the one who didn't get nosebleeds.

Nails coughed and said to her, "So, what shows do you like?"

The first few days were a joyful success, and Jeremy figured that Accumulation would, at most, take a few more. Instead of driving all the way back down to his parents' house, he'd been staying at a Whirl Garden Inn—which offered free coffee at all times and free breakfast from 6:15 – 6:17 every morning.

Jeremy hopped in his pickup and cleared out another tag sale, two Whirl Army Thrift Stores, and a very earnest student pottery sale at Whirl Region 14 High School.

And while driving back to the bridge, Jeremy smiled and talked out loud to himself. He fantasized about being hugged by smiling/dazzling executives in slim-fit suits who all kept saying how they couldn't Accumulate him fast enough.

"Where have you been hiding with all of these erection-producing ideas, dude?" they all said. And Jeremy said to the windshield/them, "Just slipped through the cracks I guess," and he pictured all of the executives cracking up at his non-joke. "Jeremy! Yeah! Jeremy! Yeah!" they chanted in his brain.

Jeremy got back onto the Sutherland-Dowd Bridge and saw a truck from The Whirl Corporation parked on the opposite side. Nails was pacing and cracking his knuckles. The Whirl Corporation side of the ScenicView Area had a professional-looking blinking sign about throwing items off. It said, "Throwing Stuff is Fun! Try It, You Dick!"

Jeremy saw the truck and the sign and the people, and he decided that he was being Accumulated—that it was all here. He thought Nails must be nervous because he didn't understand. Jeremy would become part of The Whirl Corporation now.

He tried to look carefree/calm/unsurprised as he pulled his pickup truck over, but his innards were in absolute pandemonium. Explosive/joyful diarrhea was on the horizon.

The Whirl Corporation side had lots and lots of people. Jeremy only had himself and Nails and the two women—one of whom currently had a bloody nose.

Whirl had music too. There was a pretty dancing woman in a red bikini who was thrusting her privates towards the blinking sign. They had more variety in terms of smashable merchandise — even considering all of Jeremy's new pottery which students had worked very/very/very hard on.

"Hold the phone," Nails said. "I thought *you* were Whirl?"

"Not yet," Jeremy said, and Nails pulled his shirt collar up to cover the bottom half of his face. Jeremy said, "Relax. This is a good thing, Nails. This is what we want. This gets me hired, and this gets you better property prices." Nails chewed the inside of his lip and thought.

Okay," he said. "Let's stick it to these bent boners."

"Well not boners exactly — but future co-workers who I already like."

"Yeah," Nails said. "Same."

Jeremy looked over at the Whirl side of things and then waited. And he kept looking, and he kept waiting. And then he couldn't take it anymore, and he burst over. Hiya Sandwich, a Whirl Corporation VP of Revenue Stream Development, was waiting for him. Jeremy recognized her from the corporate directory he'd practically memorized.

Hiya Sandwich said, "I know that look!" and she pointed at Jeremy's face. "*You* want to play for *our* team! Clap/clap/clap."

"Where can we work on Accumulation agreements?" Jeremy said. The Whirl Corporation was a warm blanket. He could get underneath it and finally start his life.

"Oh," Hiya Sandwich said. "No. We can take it from here without Accumulating. Why would anyone Accumulate a Non-Compliant Business? Accumulating is such a grandpa idea anyway! No/no/no. Now, we just take great ideas. And we're all really excited! This is a good one." She gave him two big thumbs up. "But you can fill out an application online for a Level One position. I would be so happy if you did that."

"But I have great ideas," Jeremy said. And he believed it. The air left his lungs, and his shoulders sank forward. This was an idea worthy of at least a Level 4 Employment Offer, he thought.

"Yes/yes/yes, Jeremy. You sure do! Look at us over here!" She motioned toward all of the action at The Whirl side of things. Then she looked across the road to Jeremy's setup. "Hi Nails!" she shouted, and she gave a big wave.

Nails was sitting on the curb, smelling his finger.

Hiya Sandwich seemed to have a very high Happiness Level.

"I appreciate you," she said to Jeremy.

"I appreciate you too," Jeremy said because he wanted to show that he could match her Whirl Positivity. It also felt really good to hear that he was appreciated — even if it was only company policy.

So he had to prove to Hiya Sandwich that this wasn't just a single good idea. He was sure that all of her 'we don't Accumulate' talk was just a way to motivate him further. He figured that she wanted to see what else he could do.

This was a test! He'd get what he wanted as soon as he delivered some more to Hiya Sandwich and proved that he wasn't a quitter.

It all made sense in Jeremy's head.

He explained it to Nails, and Nails said, "Yeah, fuck these guys."

"Well no/no/no," Jeremy said. "That's not exactly how I feel at all."

"Yeah," Nails said. "Me neither."

He went with the first idea he thought Hiya Sandwich would like. His resources were limited.

He painted a target on some plywood and glued a light bulb to the middle. Nails secured it with rocks 70 feet from the bridge. Jeremy made a sign, "Smash The Light Bulb — Win 50 Credits!"

Jeremy had crates and crates of old/cheap water glasses and coffee mugs and glass jars. He could sell them for a single Credit each. They were the perfect size to throw.

And boy did it take off! People ditched The Whirl Corporation to see what all of this bullseye business was about. It was a little after noon, and the bridge was flooded with people.

There was even a line. No one could hit the light bulb, but they tried/tried/tried.

Hiya Sandwich gave Jeremy a double thumbs up and shimmied at him.

Within half an hour, The Whirl Corporation had their own target with a blinking red light in the bullseye. The prize was 1,000 Credits.

Hiya Sandwich tapped on a tablet as she shouted, "This is another thick one, Jeremy! Love/love/love."

Jeremy shouted across the bridge, "Yeah! Miss Sandwich! Look at how we're contributing! Look at how we improve our ideas together! Imagine if we could do this all the time! If only we were *both* Whirl Employees! Right/Right/Right?"

Jeremy had to be excited for her success. He had to show that he was Compliant. And he had to be Accumulated—even if they didn't do that anymore.

They'd make an exception for him. He could feel it, and he always trusted what he could feel. Doubling down was a no-brainer.

It took Jeremy a few minutes to duct-tape old styrofoam and bubble wrap to Nails' body and fit the bicycle helmet to his head.

But before Nails could work his way down to the rocks and water, Hiya Sandwich beat him to it and moved the girl in the red bikini down below the bridge.

Middle-aged men paid to try to hit her with small lamps and gaudy vases. The girl was unprotected and dodged and darted in her high heels, letting out little involuntary screams and cries— and this only made the middle-aged men more excited. It turned out that they really/really/really preferred her to be terrified.

Hiya Sandwich copied and improved every move that Jeremy made.

She shouted across the road, "Woop/woop/woop, Jeremy! Your ideas are so FeelGood! I almost want to whisk you down to ExecBranch South—just to see what would happen."

And what else could he do?

"I'm getting thick just thinking about that 'almost' Miss Sandwich! Let's find a way to work together!" he shout-pleaded.

He was not above begging and trying. Hoops were made to be jumped through.

And not everyone carved a new idea out of thin air like he did. It was a special thing, and The Whirl Corporation could take it over and completely dominate it.

Jeremy looked at Hiya Sandwich and felt like maybe he just needed one more big idea. He was optimistic. Maybe he was *this* close. He thought/thought/thought, and then he started sending lots and lots of messages.

A rented flatbed truck, that Jeremy had ordered, eventually rolled up and parked. On the bed of the truck was a small crane and a very dead horse.

Hiya Sandwich looked at Jeremy's new item. Her eyes bounced around, and her mouth was half smile and half snarl.

People flooded over to Jeremy's side to look at the dead horse, which was just starting to bloat.

Jeremy, of course, couldn't take his eyes off of Hiya Sandwich. This was all for her.

She tapped something out on her tablet. Jeremy wondered what kind of compliments she was writing.

The auction began and Hiya Sandwich came over to outbid the highest bidder. The price went up again, with more and more people, and she outbid them all.

"200," someone shouted.

"250," Hiya Sandwich said.

"255," said someone else.

Hiya Sandwich's smile was still plastered on, but it had lost its ability to make others want to smile too.

"Enough," Hiya Sandwich said. "500." She scanned the crowd. Jeremy got the sense that she was daring someone to interfere.

There was no question that the horse had to be hers. The price didn't matter.

The WhirlTempsAreHappy flatbed operator hooked the horse to the crane with a thick strap around its neck. He hit a switch and the crane chirped alive. The strap tightened, and the horse slowly lifted off the flatbed, head/neck first. It kept rising and rising, above everyone's heads and above the cab of the truck. It rose higher and higher and then stopped — sixty feet above.

Jeremy's guts rejoiced in the fact that Hiya was so determined to buy what he was selling. He drummed his fingers on Nails' shoulders and looked on. Hiya Sandwich held up her hands to quiet the crowd, and she stood at the controls.

She raised an arm above her head, jazz-handed toward the sky, and slowly lowered her index finger to the button.

It went *thunk*. And the hanging horse started to move. The crane started to spin on its axis, and the horse circled around.

It spun around the crane faster/faster/faster until the horse was almost horizontal to the ground — its legs limp and slack and dead and forced to come along.

Jeremy was the only one capable of not staring straight up at it. His eyes moved from the spinning horse to the faces in the crowd — Hiya Sandwich's especially.

The timing had to be just right. If Hiya Sandwich released it too early or too late, the horse's body would careen off to the side and crash through the trees into the woods.

"Now!" someone shouted. "No. Now!" they said. "Now! Wait. Now!"

Sometimes people thought they knew things that they didn't

actually know.

The horse went around/around/around, and then finally, Hiya Sandwich released it with another *thunk*. The horse was off and out and over in a perfect flight. And everyone sucked in a short/quick breath.

The horse seemed to glide out. It looked like it would never fall to the ground. It would stay in the air forever, eventually flying off and spinning into the horizon.

But then, of course, it started to come down. Dead horses always do.

And it slam-thudded its weight onto the rocks and water and slid and scraped until it stopped. The crowd erupted in shriek-laughs and happy-groans and clapping.

The two nameless women threw up their arms and stamped their feet—and grimaced at the handsaw that was leaning against the dumpster.

Hiya Sandwich's eyes shot into Jeremy's. She tapped the spot next to her on the flatbed with her foot. Jeremy scrambled up. He was finally taking his place with The Whirl Corporation and with Hiya Sandwich.

He waved a big one to the crowd and blew some kisses. It felt right.

Some Whirl Officers parked and nodded at Hiya Sandwich, and she nodded back.

Two of them lunged up onto the flatbed. They pinned him down while the pretty and extremely adaptable girl in the red bikini tied his hands above his head. The crane started, and in no time Jeremy hung from his wrists, sixty feet up.

"He's been Flagged as Non-Compliant!" Hiya Sandwich shouted. Her voice echoed all around Jeremy. "Should we Eliminate him?" she said, egging the crowd on—shimmying and punching the air in front of her. Down below, the customers all cheered and clapped and recorded with their phones. Dads lifted kids onto shoulders.

And way up, Jeremy screamed with everything in his body — about fairness and sorry and ideas. The words came out of him without clear order or intention. They were just the last-ditch, panicked efforts of a Non-Compliant troublemaker who finally realized, but couldn't articulate, "I thought I knew something, but I was wrong."

Jeremy looked down and saw the hundreds of smiling/ interested faces in a tight little crowd. He'd be the first publicly Eliminated individual by a private corporation. No more closed door Eliminations. The open corporate secret was just plain open now. It could even become a New Revenue Stream — monetizing the Eliminations.

And up and out, he could see how the river bent on the horizon and how the trees parted ways to let it. The birds were singing, and a breeze whistled by.

And down at the far end of the bridge — away from the crowd and the cars and the merchandise — Jeremy saw Nails, huffing it down the road with everything he had.

THE OTHER SIDE OF THE WOMB

when they let you hold your baby   you unravel
the hospital receiving blanket   hold his hands
count his toes and cover them again   it's cold
you search your overnight bag packed for delivery
dress him in the clothes you chose to bring him home
swaddle him in his blanket   bouquet of blue poppies
find the book you read to him while he was living
still inside your belly   you take the time to read it twice
then again   and again   and again   and again
cast a spell   close your eyes   summon him
awake   still   sleeping

      when they come to take him
      you make them call him by his name

I AM THINKING OF FEEDING
MY EARS TO MY FAMILY

Because my partner says *cutting them off wouldn't work*
to quiet the noise. And so I go on and tell him how
I'd sauté both fatty lobes in coconut oil with lemon zest
and torn leaves from my brittle rosemary and basil and thyme
or cartilage with a candied glaze, served right after supper.

When our smallest child soaks in the bathtub
his ears are underwater, and after I scrub his feet
I have him stretch his arms out like an airplane
or a bird or the letter "T." He rinses in the milky bath
little bottom bouncing off the tub. His ears still hear me.
I know because he smiles and closes one blue eye
says *hmm?* smiles again, spits water, makes a face
like his father. He has just started doing this thing
where he says *hmm*, pretending not to hear.

Our older son talks constantly about everything
repeats himself to make sure I am still listening.
About what I can't remember. It's a shame I can't
remember. His limbs wiggle and shake when he talks
and look like noise, too. He tells me it is too quiet.
When I am making his sandwich with *no tomatoes or cheese*
he looks at me for what feels like a long time, tucks his chin
like a beaked animal and points with his whole body
at a photo of us at a fair in San Antonio one summer.

Where are we again? In the photo, I am in my early twenties
he and his sister are tucked close to my body
a capuchin monkey on a leash perched between them.
I want to stop him from talking. I want to tell him
I want to keep thinking about this painting I am thinking about
for once but I hate talking. Sometimes I hate listening, too.

I tell my partner in the evening, *Stop talking to me.*
Pretend I am not here. My ears close like tired mouths.
Our oldest daughter hardly speaks to me, mostly hisses.
Her splitting tongue always trailing behind her.
Her whole body long when she walks down the stairs tonight.
What is for dessert? she asks, always wanting more of me.

Granny had one dress that she wore every day.

GRANNY

Granny had the cat's pajamas. Hanging in her closet of course. Granny had a beer. Granny had one blue eye and one brown eye. She had had two boys and a girl. The boys did not speak to each other or Granny, only ever to their sister and would say, "That bitch," about Granny, or, "That asshole," about the other. My mother, the sister, talked to everyone all the way from Charlotte to San Francisco, where she ran a taco stand under the Golden Gate Bridge. At least that's what Granny said. I didn't know what my mother did because Granny never told the truth. Every time I asked her what my mother did she said she worked at a taco stand, at a stationary store, at a popular café, for a cab service but only in the office. The taco stand was what I liked. What a view it must've been! "What's for dinner, Granny?" "Crepe suzette." But it was hotdogs and potato salad. "Don't believe ever what anyone says," Granny said. "Have some more fillet mignon," Granny said. "I'll drive you to the movies but you're not aloud to kiss any boys." She laughed when she said that one. "Only men," I shot back and laughed with her. "You've been talking to your mother," Granny said, then let me out of the car. My father was a tree trunk from up north who rode a white train through midnight ghost towns, stealing the souls of bored girls. From talking to Granny when she had beer and eavesdropping on conversations, that's what I've been able to put together. Apparently he smoked cigarettes and did not know how to play the piano very well, which was a disappointment to his own father. Granny had glasses she never wore, sitting in a chair at the window, watching the road, with a magazine on her lap. "There are two Carolinas," she would say, "but there's only use in knowing one of them." "Don't worry, Granny, one day you'll run a taco stand under the Golden Gate Bridge, too." Granny had knuckles like apples. Sweet and red. They made me want to kiss all the faces they had ever punched. She didn't mean it, I would say, but you had it coming, I would say. Granny had one dress that she wore every day. But every day it was a different color. People thought it was a new dress each time. I knew the truth of that one, though. The cat's pajamas was what she was trying to put on when things started to stop working. I think she wanted to surprise me. A Sunday morning perfect for cocoa and graham crackers. I found her on the floor, half in and half out. There was not a bang or flash if that's what you were thinking. There never is. I sat on the bed and drank my cocoa as only she would tell me to do. There's no rush. Drink, sweet dear. There is no rush. And we talked. Sort of. Or rather, I guess, she talked. I listened. She told me how easy things were as long as you didn't want too much, which was very difficult. She told me to have an umbrella handy just in case of bad weather but not to let anybody know it was there so I wouldn't look like a worry wart. She told me that if I grew up tall to wear heels anyway and to hell with whoever had a problem with that, and that I should never leave a party until I was thrown out. Her head was on the floor. Her eyes were on the ceiling. There are other things out there besides taco stands, her twisted hands announced to the room, it was my grave mistake to not know that until now. Granny's wrinkled breasts pointing in different directions like strange roads. Follow one. But not the way your mother did. Please make your own way. It was getting late and things were getting quiet. Dark the way winter gets dark in the afternoon. If you ever need a touch of air in your lungs, her voice was saying, I have a small bit of breath for you that you can carry wherever you go. Take it. And put it in your chest. Near your heart. But don't use it or even think about it too much or it will blow up real big and tear you apart. It is, after all, what the sky is made out of.

JASON GEBHARDT

GRAPES

for Stanley Plumly

Perhaps for no other reason than it's February,
or that the leaves raked to the tree boxes
have been trucked out, Francis refuses to walk.
Nothing to run through, I guess. Nothing gathered
up or put away to redisperse. So I carry him.
The sidewalk already slick with a dusting of snow,
fat chunky flakes that melt at first, then pile
quickly. *Francis tree*, he says and points
to the sweet gum sapling. Decades younger
than *Madeline tree* and *James tree*, sibling maples
further along. We're off to the store for milk,
toilet paper, D batteries. Our part in the ritual
of weather. Small routines nested within large ones.
Small as each grape sliced the right, safe size.

GARY FINCKE

PENTECOSTAL

Like carefully selected wine,
preparation is often paired
with prudence, the vigilance

of a single mother's Shepherd
reinforced by motion sensor.
Coyotes, some nights, rouse the dog

to barking before frightening
my daughter's floodlight to brilliance
when it confirms their trespass,

but that evening, carrying an axe,
a neighbor climbed her stairs
to declare he would kill her dog

and anyone who tried to stop him.
The steep, empty lot next door had
been cleared of brush and damage

to lessen the chance of wildfire.
As if emptied, every nearby house
was darkened, the street fleeing

like refugees, following safety
to see where it was going.
He crouched, a gargoyle

for the unbearable, four steps
between him and the entrance
to the radius of the axe handle

he hefted slowly from left to right.
For a moment, mystery would not
shut up. Motive lived at the far edge

of language. From somewhere close,
a car alarm began to moan inside
a garage like a weakening pulse.

From house to house, barking began, each
flaring light translating those speeches,
not into salvation, but reprieve.

You didn't think it was that big of a deal, eating
a few here and there while you worked.

PURPLEST

Purple like the blackberries you and your mother picked during your first childhood summers. In the memory, you are five, bug-bitten and brier-pricked, skin salty with sweat. You trek alongside the road holding big plastic bowls to collect fruit in. Earlier, at home, your mother had laid out sterilized tongs and jars for canning. You didn't think it was that big of a deal, eating a few here and there while you worked. When your mother faces you and the empty bowl, your mouth stained and smiling, she laughs. *Was this you?* she asks. You nod. You didn't yet have the words to explain that taste: a taste so rich and sweet and sharp that you didn't even notice your hand reaching in until there was nothing left.

Purple like the skirt of leaves on your cactus. You have a black thumb, but are having a good time pretending otherwise: plants lining the inside and outside of your small apartment. You've had the cactus for three weeks. You didn't think you'd overwatered it, but when you touch it's nopales, thick with flesh and rot, they fall off. You bury the dead in the same pot. You heard the leaves of cacti will root when replanted. You watch for growth, hoping that what's already died will still somehow survive.

Purple like the sky on your way into Oklahoma. You're driving in from West Virginia. It is the first time you've left the state, your home. Lightning cracks like struck pool balls. You and your sister can feel the thunder from inside the car. You're twenty-five. You're afraid. The world is all black, save for the small eyes of your headlights. The world is all black, save for the horizon illuminated in brief flashes: god's palm opening and closing. *It's the end of the world,* you say. *The edge.* Your sister squints through the windshield. *This is an omen,* you say. Your sister keeps driving. It's been twelve hours on the road and you can barely hold your eyes open. You trust her more than yourself to keep the two of you safe. She slowly changes lanes in the hammering storm, always so cautious. The rain seems to rip from even the ground. *Yes,* she says. *But not a good one.*

Purple like the back of your throat, a dark corner carved from rushed blood and two tongues. He traces the ridges on the top of your mouth and you moan. Earlier, you'd asked him what he would change about himself if he could. He said *I'd stop spreading myself too thin.* When he asked you, you thought about lying. *I don't know how to be alone,* you'd said slowly. *I don't know who I am without someone else in the room to tell me.* He laughed and grabbed your knee, brows knit but eyes bright with humor. *Man, who hurt you?*

Purple like the bruises along the sides of your hands. You'd pounded the walls, panicked, after he stopped you at his front door. He'd held out both palms, trying to calm you down. *You're too fucked up to walk home. It isn't safe.* He, the best friend of your frat-house boyfriend. His fingers touched either side of the staircase. You felt so small. The next morning, you pulled your dress down from where it had been hiked above your hips. You remember little. You remember weeping *Let me go.* You run home, shaking, your hands throbbing. Purple. Part of you wishes you'd hit the walls harder, broken bones, had something physical to point to and say *This hurts.* You'd been split. Halved. You'd been shattered, pieces of your memory missing. Part of you wonders if you'd really asked for it.

Purple like the stuffed horse you received on your sixth birthday. Her coat was pricked with silver thread. You thought she shone like the moon. You named her Moonshine. As you grew older, you started developing little tics. You turned the faucet on with your right and left hands. You completed tasks in fours: knocking on doors, walking to classrooms, chewing. You kept Moonshine on your bed every night. If she fell off in your sleep, you believed your world would quickly begin unravelling. You continue a variation of this routine even through college. It's your freshman year when you and your friends are invited to a Halloween party. You don't have a costume and you don't have money. You do, however, have a leotard and cat ears. You have Moonshine. You don't even think about it as you saw through her thick, white tail. You cut it at the base of her hind, where the seam runs. You safety-pin Moonshine's tail to your ass and become a cat for the night. When you stumble back to your dorm, feeling for her coarse hair and find it missing, you will want to throw up. The next day, when you're insufferably hungover, anxious, and lonely, you know: you alone are your own fault.

Purple like your wine-stained birthmark. Your mother tells you when you were born the pigment stretched from head to toe, wrapped around your body like an umbilical cord. It disappeared over the following week, but you were left with a toothy, scissor-shaped mark on your right hand. You read that birthmarks are talismans from past lives. They reveal how you died, how you lived. A dagger shaped mark: death by knife, potential soldier. A fire shaped mark: death by burning, maybe blacksmith. You inspect yours. You think about death by cutting, by severance. You think about sewing, your seamstress mother. You think *Just as well*. We're all part of the world until we're not. We're all whole until someone cleaves us.

Purple like the illustrations in your favorite childhood book.

Your mother read it to you often, her voice soft and low and even. A sewing machine purr. *I Love You the Purplest*, a book about two sons wondering who is loved best. You saw yourself in both almost-men; Max and his red wildness, Julian in his blue caution. Together they become something new, beautiful. This was before your sisters were born, when your mother did, in fact, love you best, love you the purplest. Purple, you later learn, does not have its own wavelength of light, unlike red and blue. It cannot be seen on the color spectrum. And yet, it exists.

Purple like the quilt your mother made you before you moved to Oklahoma. She wanted you to have something of home, of her. You never wanted to leave in the first place. After you settle into your new apartment, you roll up the quilt and place it in a closet. Your mother who has driven eighteen hours to help you looks at you with a sadness so big you feel your heart in your throat. *It doesn't match*, you reason. She nods and leaves the room. Months later, you take the quilt out, hold it. It smells of dust and wood. It smells like comfort. You trace the seams of stars that spread across the fabric. You read that in order to make purple dye, thousands of snails have to be hunted down, their shells cracked, their bodies removed. The snails are soaked and their hypobranchial gland, the one that creates mucus, the one that keeps their small bodies safe, is taken out. The juice is gathered in a bowl and left in the sun. Under the light, it changes: white, yellow, green, purple, red, to black. Timing, so paramount. You give silent thanks to the snails and your mother. You count your blessings: cut fabric, re-sewn together. You are warm.

BENJAMIN BALTHASER

DISMANTLING

Before morning, my neighbor peels roofing tile
from a house that refuses to grow smaller in the sun.

In half-light, dry wood slides to hotpatch
like a wooden cart hissing through gravel.

One of his sons loads jets in the Indian Ocean
with bombs the black shape of a cross; the other

sleeps in a car in San Francisco, tires slashed,
windshield shattered. Who wouldn't wake up

before the light breaks to take apart your own roof,

one tile at a time? Or tie a tarp like a blanket
black with melted snow. The radio crackles

like fire. Mozart is elegant, mathematical,
precise. The news is elegant. My neighbor

gently, deliberately climbs down the ladder
his lunch steaming from a white plastic jar,

while crows fold and unfold their wings,
like black gloves in the shelves of branches.

EDDIE KRZEMINSKI

JIMMY JOHN'S

Just out of high school, we spend our shifts
breathing bread dust, spackling mayo,
gutting French loaves. My co-worker is patient
as he trains me, directs me to the meats and cheeses.

On the line he calls out the sandwiches.
I recognize the way he slurs his s's,
the halt before a consonant, the sinew
in his neck tensing like a harp string.
Sometimes he repeats the long orders,
evidence that he can say them
once without stuttering.

I wish there were time to pause
in the middle of this lunch rush
so I could clench his strong shoulder
and tell him his lips are something sacred,
that I know what it's like to live with
a throat scarved in finger-shaped bruises.

But I shut my mouth, nod, and wrap
the subs, because you can't say things like that,
not to a kid who hasn't touched twenty-one,
especially not here in a fast food joint
where such an obvious truth
would be lost to the carbonated ether
of soda machines and cash registers.

Even if I could find the time,
what if I tried to speak but couldn't?

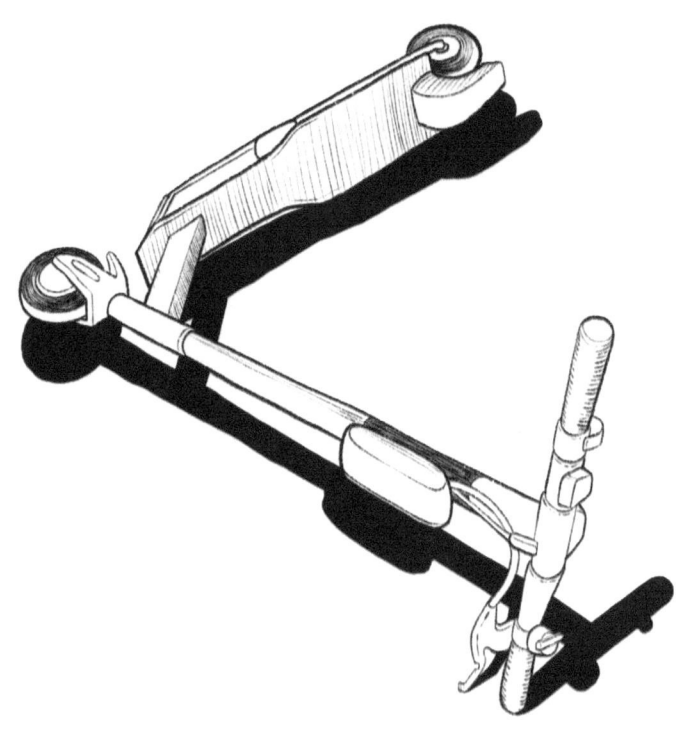

"You're right, Colin," Linda will say to me.
*"Scooters **should** be outlawed."*

DOCKLESS

I know how people see me: retiree, 69, divorced. Complains about twenty and thirty-somethings gazing at their phones. Rages against those dockless e-scooters blighting our public rights-of-way. Bitches about four-dollar cups of coffee. I'm a "true character," they say. It's not a compliment.

My wife walked out on me two years ago. She's a gastroenterologist, so there's no alimony. She took our dog and moved to Portland, Oregon to "start over again," as she put it, as if her twenty-four years with me was a pointless journey down a path to nowhere. It's now just me in a two-bedroom-and-a den condo.

One nice thing about living in a condo is you're never alone. Technically, that is. Here are the names of my fellow building residents who seem happy to see me: Clover, Moppet, Scruffy, Pancake, Bluebell. You can interact with dogs.

There is also a front desk staff: "concierge service" they call it, like we're in some luxury hotel. But it's really just the person who gives you your packages. I talk to them, they talk to me. We converse. I suspect that "engage residents" or "listen with apparent interest" is in their job descriptions. I often wonder: do they talk amongst themselves about the residents, not unlike how teachers gossip about students or orderlies in mental institutions talk about patients? God knows, there's plenty to talk about: all those millennial scooter-riders whose rich parents have bought them their condo as a family investment; all those high-maintenance young professionals who act like they're still at work bossing people around; all those cranky old retirees.

My favorite front desk person is Linda. Short straight black hair, kind brown eyes behind tortoise-shell eyeglasses. Linda used to do the overnight, but now works the 6 a.m. to 4 p.m. shift. I talk to her every morning, after my 7:45 a.m. walk down the street to get my $1.10 cup of coffee at the 7-Eleven. We have nice chats. For example, I might talk to her about scooters. How if one of those millennial nitwits plows into me on the sidewalk, they'll just go on their merry way while I writhe in a ditch with a compound fracture. How if I hit a scooter with my car, it's automatically my fault and I get 20 years for vehicular homicide while I'm simultaneously sued and lose everything.

"You're right, Colin," Linda will say to me. "Scooters *should* be outlawed." She says this with conviction, her eyes flashing with righteous anger. You can't fake that.

I think she likes me.

You get older as time goes by, but when does one cross that threshold and become officially and certifiably *elderly*. For me, it was August 3, 2007, around 7:30 p.m. I was 57 years old. For thirty years, I had played third base for our office softball team. In the summer of 2007, we had a new team manager, "Brent." I don't want to use his real name.

For three innings I sat on the grass: watching, waiting, glove on lap, being eaten by mosquitos. Between the third and fourth inning "Brent" approached me. He kneeled down so we were eye-to-eye. He spoke slowly and enunciated his words. "Now, Colin," he said, "I'm going to put you in at second base. *Is that okay?*" Like I was 90 years old! Like I was an invalid!

"I think I can manage that, 'Brent,'" I said.

We were playing some international development organization and they had this young Adonis in center field who, word had it, used to play minor league baseball. And now he's playing against a bunch of paunchy middle-aged federal bureaucrats with pre-arthritic knees. Did that make him feel good about himself? So anyway, I'm at second base, and Mr. Professional Baseball Player *scorches* a 100 mph line drive right at me. Before I could react, the ball slammed into my glove.

Thwack! *Nice catch Colin*, everyone said, with a not-so-subtle undertone of disbelief.

I was elated for about two seconds, which was how long it took for my glove hand to begin pulsating with pain. I pulled my hand out of the glove; my palm was bright pink and starting to swell. "Brent" came over and looked at my hand. He smirked. He said I might want to hold, as he put it, a "common kitchen sponge" in my hand to slip in the glove from now on to "ameliorate the impact of the ball." Assuming, he said, "that you intend to continue playing in the immediate or intermediate future."

That was the last time I ever played softball. It took two months for the purple bruise to go away. Ten years later, "Brent" was my boss, and two years after that, he forced me to retire. He reclined in his ergonomic office chair as he guzzled his coffee and told me I wasn't sufficiently productive, as compared to my younger colleagues. "Younger" was implied — he didn't actually say it. I had two choices: a humiliating cascade of counseling memos and personnel actions that would be unpleasant for everyone. Or a "glorious retirement that affords me more time to spend with my family." This, he actually said.

At my retirement gathering in Conference Room B — coffee, a box of donut holes, some cubes of processed cheese on a paper plate — "Brent" made a few perfunctory remarks. He called me a "true character" and an "irrepressible spirit." What was that supposed to mean? At other retirement parties he went on and on about how great the person's work was, about this irreplaceable colleague everyone would miss. He didn't say that about me.

Then it was my turn. At every retirement party I've attended, the retiree says the biggest thing they will miss is "the people." I didn't feel that way. Most of my colleagues were okay I guess, but I wouldn't particularly "miss" any of them. I decided to poke fun at the boss, kind of like a comedy roast. "Brent" was famous for drinking vast amounts of coffee. He had his own coffeemaker in his office and drank approximately 15 cups a day. This was the only chink in his armor, the only indication that this uber-achiever, this whiz kid, was not perfect on the many occasions when he would point out my imperfections. So I said, "Brent drinks a vat of coffee every day. A vat! He drinks so much coffee his stomach probably looks like the Number 4 reactor at Chernobyl."

The reaction was silence, a few muffled coughs. No, I wouldn't miss these people. "Brent" didn't laugh at all. He just said, with his smirk, "Yes, Colin, I *do* like my coffee."

My then-wife was at the retirement party. She looked disgusted with me. "Well, that was embarrassing," she said during our drive home.

"This coming from a woman who analyzes people's excrement for a living," I answered. "Thank you for your support."

She moved out two months later. I miss our dog.

Linda is 44 years old, 25 years younger than me. I googled her. There are websites that tell you how old people are and if you want to find out their address or whether they have been arrested, you have to pay. I would never do this — I'm no stalker. Linda is divorced (she told me this), but doesn't like to talk about it. I told her it's hard to meet people when you're divorced and an elderly retiree. "You don't look elderly," she said. "You should try dating apps like those for people over 60."

"No thank you," I said. "Back in my day, an app was something you ordered before the entrée came out."

She laughed — and it was genuine. Not at all a pity laugh. Another time I pointed out that when she was ten years old, I was 35 and we probably wouldn't be having these kinds of conversations. She chuckled, but I think it was a nervous chuckle. I regretted the words, "these kinds of." Exactly what kind of conversations did I mean? What did she think I meant?

I'll just say it: I wanted to ask Linda out on a date. Should I, I wondered? Is it "appropriate?" I considered it carefully. Would it be sexual harassment, since she works in my building? Technically, she works for the management company that our condo board has hired. So it's kind of like the condo board is her boss's boss, and the condo board represents me, a resident owner. So then: was I her boss in some technical, court-of-law sense? I didn't think so. There was nothing in the condo docs about this. I checked.

But the more important question was: what, if any, was the chance that she would say yes? If she said no, it would be awkward for us both, and how would I continue to talk to her after my morning walk? Instead of passing her in the lobby, I could enter the building through the loading dock. But even if I did that, there's a camera there and she might see me on her monitor avoiding her and what would she think?

But then, if she said yes and we went on a date and it was a disaster, well, that would be even worse. So I decided I probably shouldn't ask her out. It was a terrible idea.

Of course, I asked her out. And it was a terrible idea, but not in the way I could have foreseen.

Last week, we had our monthly condo board meeting. They are typically sparsely attended: retirees, cranks, chronic complainers. But this one was more attended than usual because the board was considering a motion that would require front desk staff to rise when an owner enters the building. It was being pushed by a thirty-something fancy-pants (again, let's call him "Brent") worried about our building's image as a "luxury" condo. He thinks that requiring front desk staff to rise upon our entrance will increase his property value when he moves out to the suburbs with his future spouse and 2.5 kids.

The board entertained comments during the "Resident's Forum" portion of the meeting. I prepared a speech in opposition.

I was quite proud of it. "What are we?" I said, my voice rising in indignation, "Kings and Queens? Emperors and Empresses? Lords and Ladies of the Manor? Maybe the front desk staff should avert their eyes when we enter the room and speak slowly with a tremor of awe in their voices! And what about the renters, are the front desk staff supposed to rise for them as well? Or are the renters second-class citizens? Maybe we could have some sort of caste system. Maybe we could brand an 'R' on their foreheads so they can be identified on sight."

And so on, in that vein. This "Brent" guy was angry. He sniffed, "that's not what this is about and you know it."

"Don't tell me what I know," I shot back.

The next morning I told Linda all about it. She loved it.

"And what are you?" I said, leaning over the front desk counter as Linda buzzed in some delivery man. "Not *you* personally, Linda. You meaning 'you people.' Chattel? Peasants? Our faithful servants? If you're going to rise, why not bow or curtsy? Does anyone know how to curtsy these days?"

Linda laughed and rolled her eyes. "Thank you for saying that last night," she said.

"I'm on your side," I said.

"I know you are, Colin," she said. Then she hesitated and went: "I shouldn't say this, but there are a lot of horrible people in this building."

My heart leapt. "What percentage would you say?"

"Maybe twenty-five, thirty percent?"

"That many! Wow!" Truth is, I had thought it was a lot higher. Seventy-five percent, at least.

Linda leaned forward. "I really shouldn't be saying this, but . . . he [meaning "Brent"] is one of the worst. He's verbally abusive. Last week, he stepped in some dog poop out by the loading dock. He accused me of not controlling the dog owners and he actually wanted me to clean his shoe. When I refused, he called me a 'useless idiot.'"

"Useless idiot," I explained. "That's a play on the phrase 'useful idiot,' which is a term that Vladimir Lenin used to describe dupes who unwittingly spread Communism." I have a Masters Degree in Soviet and Russian studies.

"Well, whatever. It was very hurtful. Part of the job, I guess."

"No, it's not. That's not acceptable behavior. What an ass."

"Please don't tell anyone I told you this, Colin."

"Don't worry! Who am I going to tell? One of the dogs?

Linda laughed. "You can tell them. In confidence."

This was a major breakthrough between Linda and me. I assume desk staff are not supposed to gossip with residents about other residents. Had the wall between the personal and the professional been breached? Had our relationship advanced to the next level?

The front desk phone rang. Linda answered. Something about an elevator maintenance appointment. The call ended.

"So Linda," I said.

"Yes?" she said, smiling. Was that a twinkle in her eye?

"I was wondering if you might be interested in going to dinner sometime, maybe an early dinner after your shift? Perhaps the Irish bar down the street?"

"Sure," she said. No hesitation or equivocation. As if there were no reason not to accept my invitation.

I decided it would be best not to leave together. People talk. Linda left at 4:00 p.m. I stepped out of our building's front door at precisely 4:10, a sufficient separation in departure time. On my walk to the Irish bar, some Millennial on a scooter whizzed by me on the sidewalk: no helmet, hair flapping in the wind, sound-cancelling headphones blanketing his noggin in a bubble of oblivious self-absorption. *Look at that prize douchebag*, I would have said to Linda if she was walking beside me: *Would it kill him to walk? Enjoy a middle age of heart disease, obesity, and sciatica, my friend!* Linda would laugh at that. My ex-wife used to laugh at my clever little observations until she stopped thinking that anything I said was funny.

At 4:30 PM, Linda was waiting for me at a table, drinking a beer. The place was empty, just a few drunks at the bar in the late afternoon. I was nervous. If this was a date, it would be my first in decades. That morning I had googled "first date tips." The number-one wrong thing you can do on a date is not listen and talk too much about yourself. You're supposed to be empathetic. Ask open-ended questions. So for example, instead of asking, "is your cheeseburger good?" I should ask, "how's your cheeseburger?" That didn't sound hard.

"Hello there, Linda," I said, sitting across from her. Say the other person's name a lot. That was another tip.

"Hello," she said. She seemed sad, subdued. Not the usual sunny Linda.

"You look very nice today." Compliment freely and often.

"Thanks."

We ordered cheeseburgers. Mine, well done. Hers, medium rare.

"I always order my meat well done," I said. "E. coli is not your friend."

She raised her eyebrows and smiled weakly. "I'm sorry. Kind of in a down mood today."

A down mood. Was it me? Was she seized by regret over accepting my invitation, thinking that if only she could go back in time and say a simple "no thank you" all of this unpleasantness could have been avoided?

"What's wrong?" I said. "Linda."

"Nothing. I'm fine." Her tone was flat. Maybe a trace of annoyance.

Our food arrived. Another beer for her, a gin and tonic for me. We ate. An awkward silence descended upon us, fog-like.

"How's your cheeseburger?" I asked.

"It's good," she said. "Thank you for this, Colin." Did that mean she was expecting the dinner to be on me? That was fine, more than fine, but did that mean this was therefore a date and not just two friends having a meal?

"Let me ask you a question," I said. "I've been dying to know, and if you don't want to answer it, I understand perfectly. Do you and the other front desk staff talk about the residents?"

"Yeah, it's been known to happen."

"What do they say about me?"

She sighed. "Colin, you've been a good friend and it's so nice of you to invite me to dinner. Please don't say anything to anybody, but I'm sorry to say I'm going to have to leave the building. I'm looking for a new job."

Oh no.

"Is it that 'Brent' jerk? Are you worried about having to rise when the residents enter? I understand. I had a torn meniscus a few years ago, and the constant up and down is the worst thing for it. Took forever to heal, but it does get better."

"No, it's nothing to do with that. I need to make more money."

"Ha, ha," I said. "Who doesn't?"

She told me that her ex-husband lost his job and the child support disappeared. The credit card debt was crushing her.

"How much debt?" I asked. "If you don't mind me asking."

She stared at her half-eaten and half-cooked cheeseburger. "Around $20,000," she said.

"Just to be clear," I said, "this dinner is on me. I won't take no for an answer."

"Thank you, Colin."

"Can you take on some extra shifts? Earn overtime?"

"That won't nearly be enough."

I took a deep breath. I knew what I had to do.

"Listen to me," I said. "As a federal retiree, I have three different pots of money: one from my pension, one from Social Security, and one from my Thrift Savings Plan, which has over a million and a half dollars accruing interest. I own my condo outright, so there are no mortgage payments. Seven years ago, I inherited $500,000 from my parents. I'm divorced, but I have no financial obligation to my ex-wife because she makes more than I do. Plus I have no children. This is just my way of saying I have plenty of money lying around and it just piles up like the junk in my second bedroom."

"Okay . . . " she said.

"Do you see where I'm going with this, Linda? I want to give you the money to pay off your debt. Not a loan, a gift. I can write you a check right now. Problem solved!"

"That's very generous, but I can't accept that, Colin."

"But $20,000 is like pocket change to me. And I expect nothing in return. Just stay. You don't have to look for another job."

She paused. "Can I think about it?"

I had a couple more gin and tonics. I was feeling good. She didn't say yes, but she didn't say no. I would give her the money freely, without conditions. We avoided the subject for the rest of the dinner. She relaxed. The old Linda returned. We talked about the other residents and she gave me all the dirt. Like how the guy in #407 got drunk and threw up in the rooftop swimming pool. Like how the old biddy in #803 called the police because she heard the television from her next door neighbor at 7:00 in the evening. We were laughing. It was fantastic.

After a couple of hours, we left. We stood on the sidewalk outside the bar. She was going one way, I the other. Our eyes met. If this wasn't a moment, what was? I leaned in for a kiss.

She pulled back, looking pained and embarrassed for us both. "I'm sorry, Colin," she said. "I can't accept your generous offer. But we can still be friends. Is that okay?"

"Of course," I said. "Whatever that means."

She smiled — sympathetically, pityingly — and patted my arm. She walked away.

I stood in front of the CVS next to the Irish bar, feeling the gin and tonics pressing into my forehead. I watched people pass by, laughing, talking, a continuous parade of strangers. I felt invisible.

On the curb in front of me it lay: untethered, fallen, splayed out like a dead animal. I bent over and lifted it up on its two wheels, this dockless vehicle, this Chariot of the Gods. I read the instructions. "Download the app" it said. I had downloaded the 7-Eleven app in order to qualify for $1.10 cups of coffee, good for any size (BTW!). I knew how to do this.

Scooter: activated. It was easy. I stepped on, one foot, then the other. My legs shook, I felt I was going to lose my balance. I crouched and arced my back to achieve a low center of gravity. It was precarious. I could have gotten off of that scooter. I could have given up, played it safe. But wouldn't I always regret my surrender? And wasn't my credit card already being charged?

I gripped the handlebars tightly. I pressed the throttle button with my right thumb and moved, slowly at first, then picked up speed. I straightened up and relaxed. I could do this, I *was* doing this. I was a colossus astride a magic carpet ride! People watched, some scattering, as if they'd never seen someone so *elderly* riding a scooter before. I could feel the wind cooling my balding head, hear that soft electronic hum slicing down the sidewalk.

I passed the 7-Eleven. If Linda were with me, she would be on an accompanying scooter and we would be riding side by side, perfectly in synch like Olympic figure skaters. Or maybe we would both be on the scooter together: me in front steering, her behind me, arms and hands wrapped firmly around my waist, her chin resting on my shoulder, her breath on my neck. I would tell her how the 7-Eleven guy always tries to upsell me a donut or a muffin. "No means no," I say to him. What does he care if I buy a donut? Does he get a commission? Five cents? Ten cents? Is that how it worked?

I glided past the Exxon on the corner. Almost $4.00 for a gallon of gas. I remembered when gasoline was 35 cents per gallon and they would give out free juice glasses or S&H Green Stamps with every purchase. Would Linda be engaged by that particular reminiscence? Would anyone?

I zipped out onto Porter Street. I would explain to Linda the ripple effects of cheap and plentiful energy, explain the geopolitics of Russian oil and gas pipelines. Out of the corner of my eye, I saw that the H-2 Metrobus had already started turning left onto Porter Street from Connecticut Avenue. Too late, the bus was coming straight for me. I panicked. I didn't know how to stop this thing. I didn't know how to maneuver. I imagined the headline in tomorrow's *Washington Post*: "Septuagenarian on Scooter Hit by Metrobus." I'm 69, not 70. Why does the press always get it wrong?

I heard the brakes of the bus screeching, the horn blaring. I saw the headlights looming, those angry eyes bearing down on me. What is it that they say? What doesn't kill you makes you stronger? I was about to find out.

THWACK! *Nice catch, Colin.*

I am crossing another threshold, lying on Porter Street, staring at the reddening sky. I know how people see me. This is how I see them: eyes glancing at screens as I talk, faces like plaster masks with their phony Potemkin smiles. What was it my ex-wife told me? She no longer found anything I said funny because "it's you saying it."

Potemkin smiles, a clever play on Potemkin villages, I would explain to Linda. But she is retreating from my words, fading, gone.

THE RECORD

"You are what your record says you are."
— Bill Parcells, famed NFL Head Coach

If history is time's only reliable mirror,
what the record says about you and me
and all the *you* and *me* and *she* and *hims*
that came before isn't likely to win wings
from any god. But then again, what gods
are there except the ones invented to forgive
our sins and provide a heaven for all the darkness
the soul claims not to see. The record shows
the soul and mind are conjoined twins,
enablers and accomplices, gods themselves
rarely answering to anything beyond the expedient.
And if any real gods still remain, exiled long ago
with their miracles and commandments, they've been
happy to stand back in the cloud of their perfection,
hands deep in their pockets century after century.
Because like you and me, that's who they are
and what the record says they are.

He ties himself to you. "Let's do this," he says.

A GRAVE FOR EVERY SHITTY MAN

"I just can't watch his movies anymore," you say. You're in your mid-tier bar, a place with metal nozzles for the booze while still offering happy hour specials that you can afford. A mid-tier bar for a mid-tier date, which is what this is.

"Really, but what about . . . ?" she says, and dangles the name of a movie that you loved as a teenager. Your resolve grows stronger, as if being bribed by a piece of cake.

"It still feels like I'm supporting his work, when I could be supporting not shitty men. Women of color, for example," you say, and you mean it.

She gives you a half-smile, which means that you're probably trying too hard. Sometimes, you do that with women who you think judge you for being a white man living in San Francisco and making the money you do and you have to assure them that you're *down with the cause*. Your politics are liberal, you explain your viewpoints clearly, but you make a self-deprecating joke that maybe it's not the time for white men to be shouting their opinions.

After you've gone through your checklist of things you want to say, your platter of opinions, you always get a little exhausted, but you try not to let that show. She goes into her upbringing, daughter of immigrants, only child. You talk about your siblings. Bring up that funny anecdote about your sisters' prank wars at summer camp.

You ask for her number at the end but there's some hesitation as she pulls up her coat and makes for the waiting uber. Maybe you're being too forward or maybe she preferred the messaging service within the app. But as she drives away, waving goodbye, you don't even bother putting her name into your phone.

It's Friday and you've taken over the end of the bar and annexed a couple stools for the six of you. But Colin is nowhere to be seen and you ask after him. There's tension in your friends' glances tonight, a skittishness that reminds you of raccoons startled by a back porch light. It's in the way their eyes dive towards their drinks until finally, Helen, pitying you, says that he's in the bathroom.

"What happened with Colin?" you whisper.

"Keep your voice down," Helen says, though you weren't shouting. "Look, after you left last week. Colin got... aggressive with Paige."

"Aggressive how?"

That's when Helen tells you that after you left, Colin said some stuff that crossed the line. She uses the word "creepy" and that stops your defense of him: he was pretty drunk that night, you think, but you don't say.

"You didn't know," she says, reassuring you like you were one of her third graders. "Just know that not everyone is excited to see Colin here."

You rock back in your step a bit. This will be later known as *the accusation* and it's the kind of dark, tendriled thing that chokes your words, always requiring you to come at it from angles for fear of slipping and being pulled down to the depths of its implication: that your friend is a predator, *a bad guy*; and you, by not shunning him, are no better. So you all wait awkwardly for Colin to get back from the bathroom and rejoin the amorous blob of people milling around the two bar stools, though now it feels like it's the amorous blob plus Colin and sorta *you* because it's your fault he's here and created distance in the group, and later, after the show is over, it will be your fault no one will want to go to Grant and Green and grab a last round.

Colin shakes your shoulder as a greeting and you nod and smile.

Thankfully, the flashing light goes on and masks the answer to Colin's question about what you were talking about. You file into the club and you're seated next to him. But you want to hear what is going on with the rest of the group now because it feels like if people are going to start getting voted off the island, you want to be on the other team. Helen leans into Tim to spread some gossip, the gossip spreading faster now that her cheeks are rosy from the two drink minimum. But her words are lost in the din of the club, and so you miss both what Colin and Helen are saying. You're there, listening out of both ears, not hearing a thing.

The comedian puts on a good set. But does Colin laugh louder than the rest when the comedian discusses how his wife likes it rough in bed? Did you detect an eyebrow arch of knowing before he hid his face in his drink? You don't know, but it haunts you as the show continues on. The vodka drowns out the soda and lime and you're left feeling a dull burn in your throat that lasts the rest of the show.

On the way out, people trade favorite lines and reveal their rankings for best live performances. You don't offer drinks and no one else does so you drift into cars that take you home. When you can't sleep, you wake up and eat a bowl of oatmeal to prevent a hangover. It mostly works, but in the morning you still feel full of bile.

You drift into more first dates. Your anecdotes and jokes are so well-worn you're worried that they've become a mirrored service that shows how boring and exhausted you truly are. So a few days later, at a bar trivia night up on Polk Street, you tell people you're taking a break from online dating — you're tired of the by-the-numbers approach. But if they have friends that you should meet, they should let you know. No one looks you in the eye when you say this.

Colin texts you to go rock climbing. You think about when to bring up the whole accusation with him. You realize it will be his word against hers. And though she has witnesses, you and Colin have history. Colin was there at your father's funeral when you were nineteen. He didn't fly back to school, and took nearly the week off. You sat in your basement and played Goldeneye for days. He didn't push you on your grief.

Now you feel like he's your dog and you have to put him down. At the climbing gym, the two of you are tethered by a rope with each taking turns going up the rock. When you reach a part of the gym where no one can hear you, you say you heard that something went down the other week and that he might have acted inappropriately.

He frowns and fidgets while making a knot in his rope. "Yeah, I mean, probably," he says. "I was pretty wasted to be honest."

You don't think that's much of an excuse and maybe that shows in your face.

"Look, you know we've hooked up a couple times? Maybe I misread the signals that night."

You *do* know their history. More than one night ended with one of them sneaking off with the other and the group's quorum broke down as a result so you got left taking an early cab home, writing a text to Colin asking him to not ditch so early next time but then deleting the message and never sending it. Or one time last March, you stumbled into Colin's apartment to pick him up and found Paige, hair feathered from bed, still half-asleep in his kitchen. So in this moment, you offer Colin a non committal response, fidget with the caribiner a bit.

"You got me?" he says, and when you nod, he ascends the rock again. Each handhold he grasps, you give him a bit more rope. When he reaches the top, you shout affirmation and lower him back down to the floor. Later, you'll repeat the process with the roles reversed. You're both reaching for the same goals, and trust each other if you fail to reach them.

Helen is promoted to associate principal of her elementary

school, so she's even harder to reach than normal. She shows up wearing a new peacock feather hair brooch and a white and red sundress. It's 8 a.m. on a Saturday, because Helen refuses to wake up later even on weekends. You're at your favored brunch place, already on your second cup of coffee.

"It's not that I don't believe her," you tell Helen. It's that you also have this history with Colin. You can't just cut him off.

"Yeah, but now it's super awkward for Paige because she can't be here when he's here."

You say that you get that, but couldn't the two of them talk it out?

"You want her to talk it out with her abuser so it isn't awkward with the group?" she asked, incredulous.

The word "abuser" stops you cold. It's one of those words that sticks to you. You can grow out of being the smelly or weird kid but if you're an abuser, it never shakes off, like a medieval version of leprosy that would see you turned out from every home.

"I don't know," you say. That's not what you meant.

"Look, I know you don't want to pick sides. Colin's been a friend to me too. But if Colin comes around when he's not welcome, I'll throw his ass out myself."

With a punk edge not completely worn off by teaching, Helen's wrath is one of the scariest things you have in your friend group. But the waitress' arrival saves you from doing the mental calculations of whatever simulated fight you envisioned between a five foot tall Latina woman and a six foot six Australian who was often called "Ostrich" in college. You still see Colin as this awkward kid who bangs his head into door frames, who seems unsure of his own strength. In the wrong light, that could be monstrous. But to you, it has always been ridiculous.

You don't get many opportunities to talk to Paige. At parties, she is phalanxed by women around her. She is a weakened animal and everyone watches her, but there's an unspoken agreement that you're not one of the guardians. At Tim's party, you see that she's flirting with Hideo again, who you know used to be in love with her and probably still is. They dated in college and are friends now but Hideo only really moved on when he met Jessie and that ended a few months ago. You don't know how to tell Hideo that Paige used to share with whoever would listen, two drinks in, about how bad a kisser he was.

"What?" Paige mouths from across the room, her brow furrowed in irritation.

But you didn't say anything.

A couple weeks later, it's getting towards Christmas. You're all out at another bar and this one looks like someone's decoration box spilled all over the walls. There's tinsel everywhere and holiday songs remixed by some EDM artist. You're flirting with the bartender with the tattoos and pixie cut but because the music is loud, she just smiles and asks you to repeat yourself and this deflates you even through your vodka fog. Colin isn't here, excised like a plague carrier. You worry that you're guilty by association, a carrier yourself now, but Helen invited you anyway. Paige isn't here and that's strange. You ask about it, and Helen says that Paige didn't feel like coming out.

"Did you hear about the governor of . . . ?" and before someone can name the state, everyone is talking about how they always thought he was a creep. "What is it about men in power being creeps?"

Hideo says they're a product of their time. "But it's a time when white men could do anything they wanted and could get away with it. And that was like all time until like, now, really."

"Hard habits to break?" Helen says and she makes an exaggerated frown. "Poor little white man couldn't figure out that other people are people. Now they claim to be the victims."

"Witch hunts!" someone says, ironically.

"Isn't it funny that the only case of people being mistakenly

condemned out of hysteria was when women were the victims?"
Lily adds. Lily is the history major of the group, though she
usually only flexes that muscle at trivia nights and with so many
caveats you tell her it's okay, she can let her intelligence stretch
out for once.

"So white boy, what's your deal?" Helen says, smiling. "Why
you gotta fuck up everything for everyone else?"

You know she's kidding, but you don't have a good answer.
"Maybe we don't know any better?" you say.

"See? Told you," Hideo says.

You all have that big rock climbing trip in Joshua Tree the first
week of March. It's been a few months now but you haven't
heard of any detente. You don't know what to do so you text
Paige telling her that Colin might show and you heard that he
was acting shitty and wanted to make sure it was okay with her
that he was coming. Paige says it's fine, but at the last minute,
she cancels. The rest of the group blames you because Colin's
there and Paige is not. You tell them that she said it was fine. *She
said she was coming.* Not everyone believes you.

You're out at the rock and it's colder than you imagined.
Snow is in the forecast, and though the sun makes the rocks light
up in shades of fire, the shade leaves the wind biting and your
breath hollow. Most of you are bundled well, bouncing around
the desert floor like astronauts in your huge down jackets. But
Colin isn't dressed that well. He doesn't have the layers. He's
grumpy and complaining about the cold but you try to ignore him
as you set the routes. It's hard work, getting up the side of a wall
when your hands are numb and the rest of you sweats. You fix a
carabiner to each anchor on the route. When you get to the top,
you fumble with the rope and have to rub your hands together
to return circulation to them. Finally you finish and Hideo lowers
you down.

The group rotates through the routes. When they don't climb, they huddle together — from the top, they look like a series of tents with heads. Except Colin, who is off cursing up a storm as he tries to do jumping jacks and stay warm.

"This is insane," he says.

"Do you want to head back?" someone asks.

He stops and his fox smile is back on in an instant. "Of course not."

The group chuckles and ignores him, but you see that this is just bravado and he's uncomfortable. He's the kind of person who would never admit to needing to go in. If there were witnesses, he'd sooner drown than wave for the lifeguard.

Thinking it'll warm him up, you offer to belay him up the rock. He accepts, and takes off his jacket, puts on his climbing shoes. For a second you can see his feet, which are pale like the undersides of fish. The word "frostbite" appears in your head, but you don't say it. Jumping and pumping himself up, Colin resembles a boxer ready to enter a ring. He ties himself to you. "Let's do this," he says.

You indicate that the belay is on and that you're ready for him. He approaches the rock assuredly, and begins to summit. As he moves across the face, he puts his left foot out for balance and reapplies chalk on both of his hands. He grabs the crimp to his right but now his weight is all wrong and you brace for him to fall. Instead he retreats to the move before. He reapplies chalk. You can see that his hands aren't maintaining their grip.

"You alright up there?" you ask. He's only ten feet away and the effect is that everyone hears you.

"Yeah, fine," he grunts, but you can tell that he's not going to make it. He tries the left handhold again.

"You want some beta?" Hideo shouts. Hideo, your climbing savant friend. Hideo who only is trying to offer advice. Colin acts like he can't hear. He tries to switch his feet and attack the chimney from the other side. But there are fewer holds that way, and he's now straining against the rope. You don't correct him, and let him try to grip his hands on the sheer face and find those holds unusable. You can hear him curse. He looks at his hands, tries blowing on them for warmth, but they do not spark fire. In the cold, they are no more useful than trying to open a door with a key of sand.

He surprises you by trying to leap for the left hold again. He grips it, briefly, and then falls away. He yelps. Looking at his now bleeding hand, he motions for you to lower him.

"Are you okay?" you ask.

"Dude, stop asking me that," he snaps. "You always ask that. It's fucking patronizing."

"I mean, I just . . . " but you stumble over your words and it sounds like an engine unable to get in gear.

He bites his finger wound and unties the rope. Before anyone can say anything, he puts a jacket on and retreats up the paths to the car. In his climbing shoes, his awkward steps echo and then fade. You feel responsible, and know that part of you is lacking the fundamental machinery to have made Colin stay. It was taken from you when you were a boy, and now you view any breakdown in male companionship as proof of what you lack. In a few minutes, you suggest to the group that they pack it in for the day.

You date. The bars and cafes are backdrops to the same set, hastily changed to give the illusion of difference. The women, too, seem to blur together like they are the same actors tasked with throwing on different wigs and costumes. Their names are different, and they talk to you about their love of travel, or jewelry making, or tennis, but there are commonalities that the actors can't hide. They all went to the Ivy League and now work in tech. They are all oldest children. No one likes *The Big Bang Theory*.

You tell your friends you would stop dating for a while because you are exhausted. The kind of tired that you feel in your bones, the kind of tired where you would need to sit on a beach for years, and only in the past, because any investment of time now was taking a pit stop when you were already behind. Your tires are bald but you have to keep going.

Soon, it's Yuri's Night, which you like to celebrate partly because you and the rest used to know a Russian named Vlad who smoked like a chimney and had a thing for photography but always, always said that some day he'd be as revered as the first man in space. So once a year you and your friends drink and celebrate Vlad and Yuri's ambitions.

This year's celebration takes place in a video game-themed bar named after a Russian character in a fighting game. Hideo picked it; it's a dark lounge with purple lighting and novelty drinks named after the character's fighting moves — "Red Tornado," etc.

You don't remember seeing Colin arrive because you're talking to an environmental attorney from Oakland. She has blue hair and you are struggling to keep her eyes on you. Eventually she thanks you for the conversation and bolts for a group of friends, who you're sure dismissed you with a glance and a chuckle.

You spot Colin from across the room. He is in a tight black dress shirt, open at the collar. He has not offered greetings to you, but instead is off talking to a group of women you don't know. The tallest among them is a blonde with nearly white hair. You know that's his type, and the rest of the group will eventually fade away to give him the opportunity to talk to her.

You've always hated the term cockblocking. It's you putting your hand, will, whatever — part of you — in front of another man's sex and saying "stop." It's both homoerotic and the definition of sexism. Both chivalric and regressive — you're stopping two consenting adults from doing whatever they want. And the blonde doesn't seem to be slurring her words, doesn't seem to be against Colin leaning in and whispering in her ear, that consensual invasion of private space.

Yet, you can't help but want to throw a verbal grenade at the scene. You want Colin to fail. You've paid a heavy social tax for his continued friendship, and the fact that he doesn't acknowledge it, has never done so, and you will not bring it up, means it must be taken out in smaller ways.

You grab him by the shoulder and say "There you are," and his mask of confidence falls temporarily, and in its place, just for a moment, you see what you think justifies what you're about to do.

You run into Paige in the cereal aisle of Whole Foods. She's wearing flip flops and idly biting her lip, staring at the back of a box of granola because of course she is—she's always been the kind of person to care about the amount of sugar in a thing and how a small decision impacts your body, your image, *you*. Seeing her now, after all this time, you think about making a joke, but swallow the urge.

"Hey, how's it going?" you offer in greeting.

She lightly smiles and adjusts a strand of strawberry blonde hair. "Fine, fine," she says and puts the box of granola in her basket. She shifts the weight from one hand to the other. She's hesitating, and you realize you're blocking her way.

"Hey, I'm sorry about . . . " and you're not sure what you're apologizing for. "I'm sorry about what happened with Colin. That's not okay."

"Yeah," she says. "Thanks for saying that."

Suddenly both of you don't want to be near the other.

"See you around?"

"Yeah."

And she walks down towards the deli.

You hope that's the end of it. You hope you're back in the "good guy" column, which is something that you hope to always be in, because the world is supposed to be full of heroes and villains and you know what side you're on. You think Colin is on the right side too, but you don't know anymore where the line is.

It's like when you were a teenager and you were trying to play seven minutes in heaven at Stacey Fielding's house. And as you stumble now, it's like being in that dark closet again and so you say sorry but you don't know where to put your hand to lean on, to find the back wall in this dark room.

Your friends don't get the memo. In fact, they seem to drift away all at the same time. People get busy, but then you see photos of them online, together, posted on Facebook. You write a message to Helen saying that you were hurt not to be included. You delete it and then decide that you have enough social capital with her to be honest.

"Hey, why didn't I get the invite to the pub crawl?"

"Sorry. Last minute thing. :("

That doesn't satisfy you but you know that pushing it further won't get you anywhere.

"Well, I miss you guys," you say. You know it sounds pathetic.

"Let's grab dinner soon," Helen replies. You know that later you'll find this text deep down in your text history, buried like a pebble in your shoe, the pain so dull and constant that you forget it's even there.

You get drinks with Colin a few weeks later. He responded to your texts, although lately it feels like the line has gone slack. You're grateful for his company when he shows, because there is his awkward gait in the door, there is his smile and slap on the back.

"What we drinking?" he asks, and it's just like old times. Thoughts of the last six months are drowned in the first round.

He's been seeing someone new. "She's cute. Owns her own cannabis business."

"Like a dealer?" you ask, somewhat sarcastically.

"No," he says, more seriously. "Like she's doing a medical cannabis delivery platform. She doesn't even smoke."

"Weird."

"She's really cool. Maybe you'll meet her one of these nights." The fact that he's saying "maybe" undercuts his enthusiasm, because why wouldn't you meet her? Are you going somewhere?

"I'd like that," you say, and try not to sound too excited. You ask about the old crew, who he's talked to.

He gives you a queer look and shrugs. "No one I guess."

You make a sound like you want to hear more and he groans.

"Do we have to do this, dude? Like, I'm just tired of the same old shit."

"How do you mean?"

"Helen is . . . sanctimonious," he says. "I know you guys are like besties but she's got this self-righteous side to her that I just can't stand. Who made her the fucking judge? And Hideo is fucking *unhappy*. Dude still isn't getting the help he needs and I'm just tired of everyone ignoring it. And Lily's . . . I just . . . I think I've outgrown them."

It never occurred to you that you could outgrow friends. You remember when you first started out in the city and you'd all go climb, then grab sandwiches at Ike's, and hang out in the afternoon in Dolores Park. You were the bright young things and this city was lit by your enthusiasm, your jokes were the best and your laughter the loudest in a city full of optimism.

"Look, we're still cool," he said, indicating the two of you. "I'm just being more selective with who I see."

"So you're pretty serious with this cannabis girl?"

"Woman. She's 31," he snapped. "Her name's Rachel. And yeah, I am."

"I didn't mean anything by it," you said.

"It's fine," he said. He takes a pull on his drink and you know that for him, by the end of the drink it will be fine. But then again, that was the old Colin. This new one has been festering resentment towards your friends for years, only you didn't know it. You worry that everyone has been similarly two-faced, not willing to share what they actually feel. In the gaps between their texts, in their absence, shadowy versions of them have appeared and none of them like you. So you talk to Colin about how he met Rachel and you recount the things they've done and you express, honestly, the idea that you want to find your own personal Rachel. That finding someone like that will keep those shadows at bay.

But later that night when you open your phone and begin swiping, you can't muster the enthusiasm to message a single person. You masturbate and go to bed.

Two weeks later, Colin messages you about lead climbing. Apparently Rachel is the outdoorsy type and he needs to recertify his lead pass.

When you embrace in greeting, you don't mention the fact that the last four texts you sent him were unreturned. That you haven't seen anyone lately, except for in passing (Paige, on the street), and Hideo (over coffee, and he had to leave early because of work). You resent that he's all smiles and oozing confidence, happy to be back on the rock after a few weeks off.

You work off some of your resentment by cleanly climbing a difficult route—full of thin finger holds and a final push up the face that looks impressive from below. Colin mentions that you look like you've been practicing. You have, you say. He ventures up the same route and has no problem clearing it. So you take him up a stemmy route, something that's going to require him to contort his body between two walls. It's something you can do but Colin, with his awkward height, will likely struggle with.

As he goes up it, you see him pause and reposition himself. For a second, you wish for him to fall just so you can have something over him. But he secures the last anchor and you let the rope out as he comes back down to earth.

"Whew, thought it had me," he says.

After an hour of climbing, you're both tired. Colin decides to go up one more route. It's a bit of an overhang, meaning he'll have to do it quickly or his strength will give out. He has no problem securing the first anchor, and give him some more rope to continue up.

But as you adjust your rope, you hear him cry out and he falls towards you. The force whips you out towards the wall and you hit it with your hand first. He dangles from the rope, now level with you, scanning the rock for where he slipped.

"Damn. I *had* it," he says, oblivious to you clutching your hand.

The irony of his mistake is not lost on you: he fell, but you got injured. You saved his life by belaying him up the rock, but for your efforts you can see red from some wound and your fingers — the pain so sharp that you feel it in the back row of your teeth — now are twisted in such odd directions that they remind you of splintered popsicle sticks.

"Oh shit, you okay?" he asks.

"Yeah," you say, without thinking. With your good hand, you lower him down to the ground. "Just next time, yell or something."

"I didn't think I'd miss the hold, dude. It wasn't planned," he says, in seeming disbelief that he'd need to say it. You know he didn't do it intentionally, but the lack of regard for consequence seems unforgivable right now, as you survey the map of blood and pain on your hand.

"Whatever," you say. You're pretty sure you broke your ring finger, maybe your middle one as well.

"Come on, say what you're going to say," he says. "You've been wanting to say it for a while."

"I mean, fuck you man," you find yourself saying, the pain in your hand sharpening your words. "You never think about how your actions affect others. You know how much I've been covering for you?"

"What?" he says, confused.

"Paige," you say.

The thing between you has surfaced and no matter how much

129

you've prepared for it, you can't stare it in the face and instead you focus on untying the knots between you. But your hands are useless as a kitten's when you have two broken fingers.

"Don't do me any favors," he says.

"I've been doing favors for you for years because that's what friends do—"

"That's bullshit," he says. "I'm done with this." For a second, you think it's climbing that he's referring to, because he's untied himself from the wall and now is taking a step away from you. But no, you know he means something larger, the contours of which can only be defined in memories of basement video games, graduation, drunken confessions, and the fact that he's always been there in your orbit, a satellite whose trajectory has gone awry.

"You're walking away? 'Cause of this?" you ask.

"For being a little bitch. For not fucking speaking to me and acting like I'm some kind of wounded puppy. So I said something shitty to a girl. Big fucking deal."

It takes you a second because your anger has smothered the words in your mouth and you fumble for air. "You're a bigger asshole than you think," you say.

He considers this and grins. It's his same fox-smile, and you know that this conversation will just slide off of him as easily as washing the white chalk off his hands.

"Yeah, maybe. But not more than the next guy," he says, and walks away.

You stand there shaking and are ashamed by how much you want to cry. You realize you're still tethered to the wall by the rope and so you pull it down. It descends quickly, hitting every anchor, before gathering like a snake in a pile next to you. You untie yourself finally and are tempted just to leave it. It's Colin's, after all.

But instead you gather it up, this thing that tethered him to you, and put it in a bag so that later, you can tell him you have it, you can make a peace offering. You're getting old: it's hard to find new climbing partners who you trust. And if Colin refuses to take back his rope, you're not sure who else is out there. You need someone to take it.

X ON FEAR & JOY

1.

X doesn't know anyone who isn't anxious at least some of the
    time, while
  Some are anxious most of the time and X wonders if
Anxiety isn't another word for fear, for fearfulness, though
    spread
  Out

  Over time, generalized, an unspecified fear of the world's
    bared
Teeth, the way disease and death and cruelty and violence are
    always
  Waiting as you pick up a piece of fruit or start down
  Stairs.

2.

But then X doesn't know anyone who isn't joyful some of the
    time, while
  Some are joyful most of the time, and X wonders if
Joy isn't another word for wonder, for openness to wonder,
    though spread
  Out

  Over time, generalized, an unspecified wonder at the world's
    open

Arms, the way we so often sacrifice for each other, help out in
   hard
  Times, give what we can, all the many instances of our
  Selflessness.

3.

X would like always to choose joy over fear; he tries but he
   finds it hard
  Work. The way sunlight filters through a canopy of trees or
Sets the late-evening fields on fire, the way the ocean beckons
   and waves
  Roar

  Or the long river of bodies flowing along a crowded city
   street, the
Chatter of language, the touch and swell — X wants it all to go
   on
  Forever and he knows it won't. He chooses joy but it's still a
  Struggle.

X & THE SPIDER

1.

This morning X kills a small black spider in the kitchen
    Sink and the insignificance of its squiggly, rudimentary
Life causes him a brief pause, a second's momentary
    Reflection.

    It's not just that little will be undone in this spider's
Absence, that not a single blessed thing of import will
    Change, rather it's the thought of death's arbitrary
        Nature.

2.

One moment this spider scurries toward sun and glistening
    Water, a tiny bubble of moisture on bright stainless
Steel that seems to vibrate in the open kitchen window's
    Light

    And the next moment it's gone, erased, nothing
Remains but a smudge which X quickly washes
    Away before going on about his everyday
        Business.

3.

Around X the countless stars soar and shout their cosmic

Noise, their immense cataclysmic tumult
Rollicking through the infinite and soaring
    Beyond

Through endless stretches of nothing through
Vast seas of everything brilliant exploding crashing
    Destroying and creating, all of it going on
        Forever.

*How irreverent of us, to use the reflection
pool to play such juvenile games.*

THE FAR-FLUNG DAUGHTERS
OF MOTHER SETON

We stop at the guardhouse at the entrance to the National Fire Academy, and I ask the guard if we can drive down the avenue. "We went to school here," I tell him, "back when it was a college."

He leans close to the car, surveying my three passengers, making eye contact with each of them. He backs away.

"I'm sorry," he says. "It's not allowed. Unless you have permission, I can't let you come onto campus. You'll have to turn around. I'll raise the barrier."

"How do we get permission?" I ask, and I'm looking down the avenue that leads to the Mother House. Beside it, the dormitory where I lived during my college years, the Pines where I played hundreds of hands of bridge, the buildings where I went to class.

"You have to contact Security," he says. "Go to the website and fill out the forms. Security-netc@fema.dhs.gov."

I start to tell him we're only here for a few days, but he's already moving away from us, toward the guardhouse.

When the wooden bar is high in the air, I drive beneath it, slowly, hugging the curb.

"Make a run for it," Mary says. "Hit the gas. What's he going to do? Chase after us?"

For a moment, I'm tempted. What fun it would be, to speed down the avenue, the guard in hot pursuit, his belly jiggling as he runs. But we are respectable women who have never been in jail or chased by security guards off federal installations. I make a U-turn and drive out onto Route 15, nodding to the guard as we pass the guardhouse.

A few hundred feet from the entrance I slow to read the sign that has recently been placed there: *On this site, St. Elizabeth Ann Seton, the first American saint, founded an academy for girls . . . it evolved to become St. Joseph's College for Women . . .*

We were teenagers when we first came to this place, we four and a hundred others, to earn our degrees. We spent our college years preparing for careers in teaching, nursing, home economics, science, and business. On sunny afternoons when our classes were finished, we walked from the Student Union building, up the path to the tree-lined avenue, then into the town of Emmitsburg, Maryland. We drank coffee at the Purple Onion, fed the jukebox so we could hear our favorite songs, and listened when the boys from Mount St. Mary's took to the stage to sing folk songs.

Now, years later, we've come back: to reconnect, to remember, and to see what changes time has wrought.

The Daughters of Charity closed our school in 1973. Four years later they sold the campus and 19 buildings to the federal government for the sum of $3,514,000. The dorms where we lived, the classrooms where we studied, the paths that we walked, all this was turned over to firefighters from across the nation who would come to Emmitsburg to learn the latest techniques in firefighting.

The local people watched the old, familiar *St. Joseph's College* sign come down and the new *National Fire Academy* sign go up. They read articles in the newspapers about the facility, and they were skeptical of what they read.

Camp David, the Presidential retreat, is just ten miles down the road. The Underground Pentagon, commonly referred to as Site R, is no more than five miles away. Fort Detrick, the center of America's biological weapons program, is 20 miles to the south. Washington is a mere 50 miles away.

If, in this secluded valley, all the government planned to do was offer classes on how to deal with fire and related emergencies, why did they need so much security? Why a guardhouse manned 24 hours a day, barricades to prevent unwanted guests, tall iron fences and armed guards to patrol the perimeter?

There's a field in a suburb north of Frederick, locals will tell you, enclosed by a chain link fence. It is a burial ground for God-knows-what, they say. Materials from Fort Detrick, too dangerous to be stored in a warehouse, they assume. Too volatile to be left unattended.

But what do country people know of the world of politics? The National Fire Academy is operated by FEMA under the auspices of the Department of Homeland Security. FEMA hires scientists to develop antidotes to poisons that could be poured into our water supply or fed to our cattle. They stockpile medicines that might save our thyroid glands in case of a nuclear attack. They provide money to state and local police forces for things like tanks, stun guns, armor-plated vehicles, bomb squads, helicopters, and drones.

At previous reunions, we've attended Saturday afternoon Mass at St. Joseph's Catholic Church in Emmitsburg. This year we've decided to drive out to the old church below the Grotto. I take the scenic route past Mount St. Mary's University. One of the two Marys in my car took courses here a few years ago, until she was laid low by breast cancer. It's been an ordeal, but she's fine now.

The Old Emmitsburg Road has changed little since our college days, but Mount St. Mary's has a footprint like never before. There are new buildings, new dormitories, a field of solar panels that provides energy for the university. Once the school admitted only men. We Joe's girls never lacked for dates. More than a few of us found husbands there. The school opened its doors to females in 1973, and now women make up 55% of the student body. Even the seminary enrollment is up. Seminarians are as off limits now as they were then.

St. Anthony's Church, just down the road from the university, has a new blacktopped parking lot. When my mother was baptized here, the parking lot was gravel. In rainy weather it turned to mud.

I've never been inside the church. When they built the new Route 15, traffic engineers eliminated the sharp turns in the road. In doing so, they relegated St. Anthony's to a back-roads, back-woods, poverty-stricken place of worship ministering to an impoverished congregation.

But no more. The village that surrounds the church has become prosperous. Parishioners regularly fill the collection baskets. The priests have money to repoint the fieldstone exterior, paint the wooden window frames, sand and varnish the double doors.

Most of our group, and there are twenty of us who have come to hear Mass, sit near the back. It's an old Catholic thing; leaving is always easier if you're in one of the back rows. I'm drawn to the front of the church. I walk down the center aisle, thinking of my mother. I want to be near the spot where she was baptized. The two Marys, Kathryn, and a few others, follow.

We find seats not quite at the front, but close. When the priest begins his sermon, I'm thinking of my mother, dead now for ten years.

Pope Francis has called for a new "balance" in his church—less emphasis on sexual matters, more on opening our arms to those who have been shunned. The priest warns us, in his homily, of the media's penchant for picking out newsworthy fragments from interviews with the Pope, and missing the broader message. While Pope Francis might seek a "new balance," basic moral teachings have not changed, he says.

Some in our group disagree. They fidget in their discomfort. They flip through the missalette that contains the Sunday readings. One of the Marys nods off.

I am thrilled to be in this place where my mother was brought when she was an infant. She was born on Christmas Day in 1912, a half-orphan. Her father had died just six weeks before. He'd slid off the road and gone over a cliff in his new Ford automobile. He spent a month in the hospital, endured a surgery that failed to fix his "twisted spine," and was sent home to die. Which he did, six weeks later.

The Daughters of Charity visited my pregnant grandmother shortly after the funeral. They offered to take some of the children off her hands. They especially liked the two little girls, aged two and five.

Their names were Ruth and Irene. Ruth, at two, was a miniature version of her mother: dark hair and eyes, a certain regal quality about the way she held her head. Irene with her red hair and freckles looked more like her dead father.

Margie, my grandmother, gathered the girls close to her. She thanked the good sisters for their offer, but she couldn't think of separating the family. Somehow, she'd manage. She was not destitute; her husband owned a sawmill and a tile factory. There were mountain lots she could sell. The boys were too young to go into the woods with the sawyers, but in time, they would be able to contribute to the household finances

The Daughters were disappointed, but they left, promising to come back if Margie should change her mind.

Spring would have come to the valley before my grandmother could make her way down the mountain with her Christmas baby and present the child for baptism. To be in this church now, all these years later, is an emotional experience for me.

The interior is freshly-painted and richly-appointed. I wish it were not so. I yearn to know what it looked like the day my grandmother brought my mother here to be baptized in the faith I have given up.

If I felt something from the priest who is saying Mass, if I sensed in him compassion and sympathy for the people in the pews, I might approach him when Mass is over. I would ask him to tell me what the church was like a hundred years ago. Does he know of any pictures that might still exist? What of the fire that destroyed the parish records, and took away from me the chance to learn who might have been there the day my mother was baptized, who were her godparents, who promised to protect her from Satan's wiles?

But what I feel from this priest is a brusqueness, a barely hidden anger at the changes he sees coming. This is a man who wants to preserve a system that has failed many of its believers. He will not care about my connection to this place, or that I yearn to know things I never before realized were important to me, and that inside I am trembling. Ten years she's been gone, but once she was here, dressed in baptismal finery, presented to a priest who poured water over her head and anointed her with the oil of salvation.

When Mass is over, I linger for a moment in the vestibule at the back of the church, looking toward the altar, imagining my grandmother at the baptismal font. She's holding the baby she delivered and carried down from the mountain so that the sin of Eve might be removed from the child's soul.

Each of us who has come back to this place grieves, in her own private way, for how things used to be, before the Daughters of Charity closed the college and sold the property to the federal government. Three and a half million dollars was a lot of money in 1977. The Daughters used it to build a Provincial House of mammoth proportions. When it rains, the building sheds so much water nearby streams overflow their banks. On occasion the runoff threatens homes that have been here since the town was founded.

Elizabeth Ann Seton was given the land in 1819. When she had no money to pay the property taxes, James and Joseph Hughes, ancestors of mine, gave her the funds she needed.

James Hughes fathered Teresa who bore Cecilia who gave

birth to Mary Estelle who was my paternal grandmother. When my father was born, Mary Estelle gave him the middle name "Hughes," in honor of her great grandfather, James Hughes, the man who helped Mother Seton in her hour of need.

My daughter Kelley was born on August 28th, Elizabeth Seton's birthday. There is a tradition in Emmitsburg to name girls born on that day "Elizabeth." The Daughters of Charity host a special Mass and birthday celebration for all these Elizabeths every year. I am not invited to these birthday fetes, nor is Kelley.   I followed my grandmother's example and gave my daughter my father's middle name which was her great great grandmother's maiden name. If it embarrasses her — having "Hughes" for a middle name — she has never mentioned it.

To remember your ancestors and the things they did is a fine thing. When traditions conflict, as they sometimes do, you must choose which one to follow.

There's time after Mass to visit the Grotto of Our Lady of Lourdes, a natural amphitheater in the mountains above Mount St. Mary's. From the church it's a short drive up the mountain to the parking area.

Beside the path that leads to the Grotto, there's a massive statue of the Virgin Mary. She stands atop a tall column, her arms outstretched in the universal gesture of giving. Mary is showering her graces down on the people who live in the valley.

Years ago, someone shot through her hand. The bullet pierced her palm like a stigmata. The statue has since been repaired and repainted. I linger beside my car, looking up, wondering if I might see some remnant of the wound. But Mary is so far above me I can discern nothing.

We follow the path through landscaped woods up to the replica of the Lourdes Grotto in France. We climb to the crucifix, peek into the chapel, visit the Grotto pool. Some who came before us threw dollar bills into the water. They've sunk to the bottom.

Kathryn has a supply of singles she's willing to donate to the cause. We crumple them and sling them out across the water. Some sink faster than others. Why, we wonder. We take more bills and wrap them around sticks, pebbles, coins. All sink, though at different rates. One of our science majors provides a possible explanation: the paper used by the U.S. Treasury contains cotton and linen fibers. The government used to buy old clothing and linen from rag-pickers. In a complicated, multi-step process they churned the rags into paper. Depending on which fibers were most exposed to the water, which would be determined by how we folded our bills, some would become waterlogged faster than others.

How irreverent of us, to use the reflection pool to play such juvenile games. Miracles have happened here. Prayers are answered. Barren women conceive. Broken hearts are mended.

We have dinner at the Carriage House in Emmitsburg, a few blocks north of the National Fire Academy. Kathy has arranged for a private dining room and a U-shaped table so we can all join in the conversation: Jenny, Virginia, Carolyn, Mary, Maeve, Patty, Nora, Barbara, Josie, the other Mary, Kathy, Chrissy, Ann, Hannah, Connie, Margo, Katie, another Ann, June, yet another Mary, Bridget, and Patricia.

We order wine and mixed drinks, and we sing our class song, several times over, stumbling over the words, making them up when they fail to materialize. Someone remembers a ditty we chanted as we walked across campus. We all join in:

> I don't want to join the convent,
> I don't want to be a nun,
> I'm a member of the Ku Klux Klan,
> All out for parties and fun

What did we know of the Ku Klux Klan back when we were such innocents, and we lived in this valley surrounded by high mountains, protected by the Daughters from the evils of the world? We knew only what our teachers told us—that the Klan was founded shortly after the Civil War, a resistance movement against Republican reconstructionists. It died out after a few years. In the 1920s it came back with a vengeance: cross-burnings, marches, lectures and rallies. Klansmen were WASPs: white, Anglo-Saxon Protestants, and they wanted America to reflect both their looks and their values. They hated blacks, immigrants, unions, Jews, and Catholics.

Why Catholics, we wondered? What had we done?

The Klan believes we owe allegiance to the Pope, our teachers told us. They say we have separate schools where our children are indoctrinated into the ways of the faith. Because of our loyalty to the foreign "ruler" in the Vatican, we are potential enemies of the state.

It sounded very serious.

But we were still in our teens. We lived by rules laid out by the Daughters of Charity. The Mount boys must be off campus by 9 p.m. Lights out by ten. You may walk into town on weekdays between two and five in the afternoon, but first you must sign out in the book in the Student Union building and sign back in when you return. If you are late, there are penalties. You are not allowed to leave campus on weekends without permission.

Maybe the Klan could help us loosen some of the rules. Maybe their parades and rallies would be fun.

Except it was all talk. No Klansman ever found his way into our valley.

And the Daughters were not without sin. We'd heard of the nun from South Carolina who nursed the wounded at Gettysburg, smoothing the brows of Johnny Reb, and spooning soup laced with rat poison into the mouths of Northern soldiers.

Even in our protected valley, there were glimpses of a changing world. For the first time in the history of our nation, a Catholic won the Presidency. The fields around Emmitsburg were white with snow when Eisenhower drove past our school en route to retirement at his beloved farm near Gettysburg. We stood at the end of the Avenue, 120 strong, freezing in our caps and gowns. The windows of his limousine were dark, but we saw him raise his hand to us, and we cheered for him, and some of us threw our mortarboards into the air.

Kennedy invaded Cuba and suffered an ignominious defeat. To prevent the spread of Communism, he sent Special Forces to Vietnam. Then he flew to Dallas, the cavalcade entered Dealey Plaza, and our Catholic president was gone. The Daughters hired buses to take us to Washington for the funeral. We stood on Pennsylvania Avenue and watched the cortege pass, and there was no music, only drums. The riderless black horse with empty boots set backwards in the stirrups was skittish, and his metal shoes sang out as he clip-clopped along that wide thoroughfare.

We returned to Emmitsburg that night, as sober as the nation. The valley did not seem such a safe place anymore. The ROTC cranked up at Mount St. Mary's, and the boys we loved answered the call. Some went off to fight in that foreign land. Some would return heroes and some broken men.

We got our degrees and went out into the world: nurses, teachers, social workers, secretaries, salesclerks, wives, and mothers. Some of us went to graduate school. Two entered the convent. One joined the Peace Corp.

An eternal flame burned over Kennedy's gravesite, and the filibuster against his Civil Rights legislation went on for 54 days before it finally passed. President Johnson escalated the war until we had 500,000 troops in Vietnam. Dr. Martin Luther King was assassinated at the Lorraine Motel in Memphis, and Bobbie Kennedy was gunned down two months later at the Ambassador Hotel in Los Angeles. Charles Manson sent his followers on a killing spree, and we were losing the war in Vietnam. Had the world gone crazy?

Our faith would protect us, we'd learned in our college years, but it seemed not to be so. We married for love, but love had its limitations. Some of us walked down church aisles already pregnant, and the shame of that hung over the marriages. Some had affairs. Some filed for divorce, and when it was granted, they began the long, arduous, dehumanizing attempt to get an annulment. To have an abortion was a mortal sin, deserving of the eternal fires of hell, but there were a few among us who, in desperation, sought out doctors known to be accommodating. Or old women who knew of potions that would bring on menstruation. Or friends who advised bathing in scalding water, drinking pennyroyal tea, running up and down stairs. When all else failed, there was no choice but to carry the baby to term.

If my grandmother saved the christening dress my mother wore, or Mary Estelle the baptismal outfits she'd used for her daughter or either of her sons, they've been lost. But it hardly mattered. When it was time to baptize our first daughter, my husband, a Mount St. Mary's graduate, and I chose to have the ceremony in the park. We belonged, at the time, to a group of disaffected Catholics who no longer felt comfortable in the ornate and spacious churches for which Nashville, Tennessee, is famous. A wooden pavilion in Percy Warner Park presided over by a sympathetic priest suited us better.

Winters we gathered under whatever roof we could find. But it couldn't last. Our priest was ordered by the bishop to spend his Sunday mornings in more churchly places. In those troubled times — pedophilia scandals and coverups, agitation for priests to marry and for women to be admitted to the priesthood — we'd begun to feel, if not unchurched, at least drifting in that direction.

When I brought my second daughter who should have been named "Elizabeth" home from the hospital, and I looked into those clear, blue eyes, I rejected the idea that her soul was black with original sin. It seemed an outrageous thing. She lay in her bassinet in our sun-filled bedroom, dressed in soft cotton shirts and embroidered gowns. On the bottom shelf of the bassinet were the blankets and crocheted sweaters, hats, and socks, all the things I had collected for her. Who could believe she was anything other than pure and clean and unspoiled? What unfeeling person, what power-hungry dictator, what autocratic ruler had invented the idea of a mark of Satan on every child brought into the world?

This child, this baby we'd named Kelley, would not be baptized. I would not let a priest pour water over her head and make the sign of the cross on her forehead, as if she needed to be cleansed of some terrible sin. She did not.

Nor did my grandmother, who waited until spring before arranging for her daughter's baptism. I remembered my mother telling me that Margie was not welcome in that little church until forty days after she'd delivered her child. Some Old Testament thing, my mother thought, about women being unclean until their bleeding stopped.

Because of the cold and ice and snow, Margie would not have wanted to leave her house for those forty days anyway, so she probably didn't mind. But I did. I minded very much.

On the last night of our reunion, we gather in our hotel lounge for a nightcap that becomes two or three. No one is keeping track. There's a freedom here we don't often feel, and we want to savor it. There are no husbands, lovers, children, companions. No laundry to do, no meals to prepare. We feel closer to each other now than we've ever felt before.

Someone always brings a yearbook, and this year is no exception. We page through it, sharing information, wondering about those who are lost.

Eileen moved to San Francisco, changed her name, then disappeared. No one knows what happened to her.

It's a shock to learn of the one who is gay, and I understand why she won't ever come to a reunion. Even after all this time and all these life experiences, there are those who would shun her. I wish it were not so. She always seemed so lonely when we were in college: no close friends, often walking alone to class or to meals.

This is Julie's first year to attend. She's been married and divorced, lives alone now on an island in the Chesapeake. On weekends she kayaks the bay waters and she's content. Texas, where she lived with her cowboy husband for twenty years, never agreed with her.

During a lull in the conversation, Julie asks if anyone has been in touch with Sister Mary Margaret. There's never a year that we don't talk about our beloved English teacher. She fled the convent shortly after we graduated, went to the Far East to study Asian culture, wrote books, and returned to the States to teach in some of the most prestigious universities in America.

She's living in a retirement community in Greensboro, North Carolina, I tell Julie. Mary and I planned to visit her a few years back, but it didn't work out. I'll send you her email when I get home. She'd love to hear from you.

Betty's cancer has returned, second time around, but she doesn't seem concerned. Maybe she'll get lucky and beat it again. Not so her husband, whose cancer has metastasized.

We cheer for Maeve who tells us how she took her cheating husband to the cleaners: house, alimony, child support, college tuition for all five kids, half his retirement, and half his investment portfolio. No matter what the Church said, what the Daughters said, what the Pope said, she simply couldn't go on living with a man who'd been in bed with half the nurses in the hospital where he worked.

The bartender has gone home, but the wine bottles on our tables have multiplied. Maeve fills her glass and goes on with her story. She met a man, fell in love, gave up her alimony to marry him.

Carol's husband came back from Vietnam a changed man. Try as she might, she couldn't live with him. The last she heard, he'd developed Agent Orange cancer on both feet. It's a slow-killing cancer, and the surgeons have so far been able to keep one step ahead of it.

The girl behind the desk in the lobby brings in a plate of chocolate-chip cookies, still warm from the oven. We come here every year, and they like to take care of us. But cookies don't mix well with wine, and the storytelling goes on.

Cynthia left the convent and went to work in a bank. When Bobbie called her this year to invite her to the reunion, she asked to be taken off all lists, never contacted again. We don't know why. She didn't say.

We are a fun group, we insist. We would never ask questions that would be hard for her to answer. We fill our glasses again.

Katie admits to having slept with six men. Six, and that's not counting her two husbands. She shrugs. As if it's not unusual for a cradle Catholic raised by Catholic parents educated by the Daughters of Charity to have taken lovers. She teaches art history at a community college in upstate New York. The opportunity was there, and she took it. With no regrets.

"Who were they?" Jenny asks. "Colleagues? Students?"

Katie shrugs. "Some were colleagues," she says, and there's a smile on her face that says she's remembering one who was special.

"But not all?"

She sits back in her seat, and it's clear she's in deep concentration. She looks up at the far corner of the room, twists her mouth to the side, taps on her cheek, chews on a finger, brushes back her hair, sits forward. "Not six" she says. "Seven."

Pause.

"No, eight"

Another pause.

"Nine," she says. "I almost forgot that one."

When she gets to eleven, she's satisfied. She's remembered them all.

The room is quiet. The girl at the desk in the other room is busy with paperwork.

"Eleven?" one of the Marys asks.

She nods.

"Seriously?"

She raises both eyebrows, wondering, not about the question, but were there more.

"Do you remember them all?"

"I do," she says. Pride in her voice.

"Were some better than others?"

"Oh, yes. Definitely." And she shivers in delicious remembrance.

"You should write them down. All their names. Do you remember them?"

"I think so," she says. She sips her wine. "And you're right. I should write them down. I might forget."

"One was black," she adds. She looks around at us, a knowing look on her face, and she giggles. "Yes, it's true," she says. "The thing they say about black men. Absolutely true."

We loved her back in college for that ringing, belly laugh, and we love her even more now for her honesty and her devil-may-care attitude. And for the gift she's given us.

The stories go on, the confessions, the falls from grace, but the priests who would hand out the penances have all gone to bed. The hotel guests are asleep, but we stay on. This is our last night. There are stories yet to be told, wine bottles to be uncorked, depths to be plumbed.

In the morning I say goodbye to my friends, drive to Baltimore and board a plane for Nashville. When I'm high above the earth and miles away, I think of the confidences I've been given, and of the friendships I've renewed. I am amazed, as I've been on previous occasions, that so many still cling to their faith. But it's a different faith now. We no longer accept the judgments of men who stand in pulpits and lecture their congregations on what is right and what is wrong.

I think of how Sister Mary Margaret's flight from the convent gave us all the courage to leave our own convents. It is a process that still goes on, that casting off of prohibitions, inhibitions, bonds of servitude.

And I think of the two little girls who were my mother's older sisters. If my grandmother had let the Daughters take them that December day, what would have been their fate?

It would have been cold when the Daughters came up that mountain road. Margie was big with child. Worn out from nursing her dying husband. The pregnancy. Six mouths to feed. Four boys, two girls. She wouldn't have known the child she was carrying was another girl.

Had she agreed with what the nuns asked of her, she would have gathered her daughters' clothing, selecting only the best, laying aside the items that no longer fit or needed mending. She'd have dressed them in their Sunday best. She would have hugged them one last time and waved to them as they walked with the Daughters to the waiting buggy.

When she passed the grounds where Elizabeth Seton once walked, she would surely have fought the urge to go up to the door, and knock on it, and ask that her children be returned to her. Had she done that, the Daughters would have explained that the girls were so much better off in their care. At the convent they would have regular meals. They would go to school. When they were 15 or 16, they might decide to take vows of poverty, chastity, and obedience. They would be able to stay there, in the convent, for the rest of their lives. Fed. Clothed. Chaste. Obedient.

As it happened, those two little girls the Daughters wanted to adopt became my mother's best friends, and they remained so throughout her life. Irene married a man who owned a construction company. When she was old and widowed, she gave shelter to a homeless man who somehow found his way to her door. He built a boat in her back yard and sold it for the then princely sum of $15,000.

Ruthie married a man who, with her help, opened a shoe store in Gettysburg. She had three children who all resembled their grandmother Margie.

Irene and Ruthie visited my mother often, and she them. It pleases me, to remember that.

CONTAINMENT

What are these houses? Boxes closed on pain.
Their discipline is like our daily walk,
which trudges past, turned courteously away.

Nothing in public speaks about the pain.
Traffic ignores it. Dry leaves cartwheel by,
a seasonal circus. Solemn-eyed facades,
right-angled rectitude and pillared stature
confront the street in silence. The back alleys
practice their self-control, recycling bins
holding things in, under the porcelain-blue
lid of the heavens, while the churches' chimes
in hourly disagreement try and try
to say what order means, or used to mean.

What pain? No one need specify. You know.
Daily it bleeds itself into the ether
in trillions of small thumb-pecked cries of anguish.

Where do they go? We need a fantasy.
Say that the pain seeps from the buried wires
into the earth. Say it becomes the ochre
that lights the gorgeous, operatic dying
of all these front-yard maples, flailing gold,
screening these upstairs windows, lest we see.

AFTER THE GREAT SICKNESS, WE GO OUT AGAIN

Little has changed. The slush-bound buses plow;
the homeless sleep in rumpled ever-presence
on light-rail trains, elucidating how
little has changed. The slush-bound buses plow.
Pigeons whose green-and-violet iridescence
rainbowed our former mornings rainbow now,
tangling our steps in bob-and-coo. The essence
of plod's unchanged. Through plod, the buses plow.
The homeless sleep in rumpled ever-presence.

Through the zoom, I saw two pasty white bodies
scurrying behind a tree, a blanket disappearing.

ONCE IN FLORENCE, ALABAMA

Before I left Chicago, I got a crew cut at the gay barber shop on Halsted. Theo spun me around in the chair, his fingers pressing his lips. He displayed me to the rest of the shop like a prize, and yelled, "Look at this beautiful boy I've created!"

No one cared. The place was full of smooth, real, beautiful boys. But I smiled at Theo through the mirror, gave him my playful seductive glare.

He grabbed his water bottle off the counter, and fanned himself. "Jesus, girl, if only you had the equipment to go with that look."

I laughed, shifted my legs, felt a tightness in my thighs.

My girlfriend, Barb, said I was in gender crisis. She read some book and a ton of blogs and started talking about Trans Pride. She said it was cool and she loved me and I should go to therapy and face my issues.

I couldn't afford a therapist and I'd never thought I had issues until Barb started harping about gender identity all the time.

"Maybe you need a vacation," Barb said, one night after we'd had a huge fight. Which I took to mean: *Go away for a while. I'm sick of you.*

So, I decided to take a long drive and clear my head. Old-school road trip. Chicago to Miami traveling only the back roads. Two-laners cutting through small towns, miles of bean and corn fields, thick back woods. I loaded my Toyota with nothing but clothes, a cooler, and my camera.

When Barb and I met, she was married to one of my professors at Northwestern. He was too old for her and I told her so, sipping warm beer out of a plastic cup at a campus party. I was in the Ph.D. program back then. Electrical engineering. Dropped out three years ago, right after I moved in with Barb. She owned a gallery on Michigan Avenue. She got manicures, shopped at Saks Fifth Avenue, and loved the ballet. I started taking photographs of her. Then other things. I sold a few, and she encouraged me. She said I had a unique vision, a complex perspective. I just liked the feel of the camera in my hand. Watching.

Barb divorced her husband for me. Most of her friends are lesbians now. She just seemed to erase her old life, as if it never existed.

"Happiness is easy," she told me. "Just be who you are, and don't look back."

That was Barb. Her life was a series of sharp fast turns handled as easily as a professional race car driver. She always got what she wanted, and it was hard not to hate her for that.

The air conditioning in my car died sixty miles south of the city, so I rode with the windows down, sun scorching my arm. The first stop I made was at a state park in southern Illinois. It was a Tuesday afternoon and the place was deserted. Biting into peanut butter on white bread, I scanned the nearby woods. Birds chirped in the trees but didn't show themselves.

After lunch, I took my camera and walked into the forest, crunching twigs with my Doc Martens. The boots were too heavy for summer, but I liked the heft they added. Enveloped by greenery, I thought of all the potential poisons: ivy, oak, rattlesnakes. I spat on the ground then glimpsed a wild purple flower near my toe. Groundcover had taken hold; there was no way to proceed without crushing the buds. I brought the viewfinder to my eye, zoomed in close and shot. Capturing the purple blooms on film then crushing them with my boots. I stopped and zoomed closer to one of the blossoms until I saw nothing but a speck of white on the stigma. I put the camera down. I'd reached a clearing, and as I emerged from the woods, the air glistened around me. Everything lightened. I turned back and snapped a picture of the brushy exit. Then capped the lens and walked back to my car.

Barb never understood me. I didn't want to be a man. Didn't want a surgeon to slice me open, change my body. I was masculine, yes. Never felt comfortable in women's clothes. My voice was thick and heavy (sultry, some women said), my jaw square. Even with shoulder-length hair I was Sir'ed by the slightly distracted. I didn't mind it. What unnerved me was when they realized their mistake. Second glance catching the fullness of my chest. Their embarrassment, sometimes anger.

No problem, I always said. No problem.

A few hours after lunch I stopped at Kentucky Lake just south of Paducah. I parked near a boat ramp, headed toward a wood plank dock. I focused my zoom lens across the lake but couldn't see the other shore. Nothing but grey glistening waters, and stillness. I scanned the water's edge, close to the dock, and heard a giggle. Through the zoom, I saw two pasty white bodies scurrying behind a tree, a blanket disappearing. Teenagers. A boy and girl, fumbling around naked under a bright blue sky.

I relaxed my grip on the camera.

Ginger had been my first. We were sixteen. She was a cheerleader, and her twin brother Henry was my best friend. All through football season, Ginger lingered in my car on Friday nights when I drove the two of them home after the game. She kept talking long after Henry'd gone inside. One night she touched my thigh, and gave me a look of invitation. Two days later we had sex in her bedroom, no one else home, the door locked just in case.

The first time I tried to touch her at school, she pushed me away. It was okay in the dark, she said, but she wasn't a lesbian. She liked boys, and she wanted a normal life.

She wasn't the last girl to tell me that. And somewhere, after the third or fourth time, I stopped falling in love and focused only on the sex, which I never lacked. The girls who liked me didn't have a problem with the sex; it was loving me that disturbed them.

My identity seemed to challenge theirs.

Barb said I'd never be able to truly love until I accepted who I was, and made myself whole. I suspected it was her, though. She really wanted a man, like all the others. She was just too stubborn to admit it. Truth is, I didn't know what any of that said about me. Except happiness was hard to find.

I watched the teenagers get dressed on the shore. They embraced. The boy's arm fell to the girl's waist. She laid her head on his chest, stroked him in the sunlight. I snapped a photo.

Back on the road, Kentucky gave way to Tennessee and the terrain turned hilly, then mountainous. Roads winding up, then down. I leaned my head toward the open window, feeling the temperature drop as the elevation rose.

About an hour from the Alabama border, I had to pee. Thirty more minutes of driving and nothing but single pump gas stations and shacks for restaurants. I pulled into the parking lot of a clapboard convenience store called Downey's. A sun-weary man stood by the door, his face and grey trousers blending into the weathered storefront. He spat a brown stream of chewing tobacco as I got out of the car, then gave me a cautious smile. I wore a White Sox cap and dark sunglasses. My T-shirt was loose, but not enough to hide my breasts. I turned away from him as I walked past, felt him staring.

Inside the place reeked of sour milk and the floor was caked with dirt. The woman behind the counter looked like Grey Trousers' twin, only heavier. At least three hundred pounds.

"Restroom?" I said.

She barely looked at me, and said, "Men's room's around back."

I swallowed. "And the Ladies'?"

Grey Trousers was behind me. "Where you from, girl?"

"Charleston," I said, filling in the twang I'd lost years ago.

"Plates say Illinois."

I took off my sunglasses, pushed my hat back on my head. It was more feminine than exposing my crew cut.

"Living up there now," I said. "Born and raised in Carolina."

"Ladies' room's inside," the woman said, then pointed toward a door in the back.

As I walked away from them I became conscious of my heavy boots, the boyish swagger of my hips.

There were two stalls in the bathroom: one toilet was broken, the other was occupied. I stood staring at myself in the mirror, fingers on my jeans zipper, feeling dislocated. Growing angrier about it as the pressure on my bladder increased.

I heard her voice before I saw her. Gravelly and raw, screaming "Fuck you, fuck you, fuck you, you grimy fucking bastard!" Then the girl stepped out of the stall, slammed the cell phone against the sink. She had short-short blonde hair which looked as if it had been hand-chopped with pinking shears, in a hurry. She was thin and tall, but not slight. She wore a lime green leather motorcycle jacket and a red heart tattoo on the back of her neck. I imagined that wasn't the only one. When she caught my eye, she stopped, slipped the phone in her pocket delicately, and smiled at me. She washed her hands, and as she dried them, she said, "You alone?"

"Excuse me?"

"You — where are you going? Who are you with?"

"Florida. Nobody." I said without thinking, not sure why.

A strained looked came over the girl's face, as if she were solving a complex math problem.

I opened the stall door and stepped in. "Sorry. I've really got to go —"

She dropped her paper towels in the trash. Her movement was strikingly feminine, though her clothes, her face, her presence, was not. She stared at me through the mirror.

Then she shook her head, and said, "Jesus, I'm cracking up here. Sorry."

The stall door wouldn't close completely, or lock. I had to go so bad I dropped my pants and peed, letting the door swing ajar.

The girl paced in front of the sink. When I came out she looked calmer. Her hair was damp, as if she'd run her wet hands through. I placed her as mid-30s, maybe younger, but she wore hard times under her eyes, watery and blue.

"Are you okay?" I asked.

She nodded. "Can you give me a lift? Just back to the main highway. Somewhere civilized enough for a McDonalds or God help me, a Starbucks."

There was laughter, loud and male, right outside the door. The girl took her cell phone back out of her pocket, looked at it. Then she twitched her head quickly, and said, "Forget it. Forget I said anything."

She grabbed a backpack off the floor. It was covered in mud and dark stains. This girl wasn't local. She was a displaced city dweller like me, I was sure of it. And at that moment my fate felt inexplicably connected to hers. I didn't know what kind of trouble she was in, but I knew I was crazy when I said, "Which way are you headed?"

She met my eyes with surprise, then shook her head. "No. You should get the hell out of here. You're a nice boy, I can tell. My shit is the last thing you need."

It took me a minute to register what she'd said. She called me a boy in the most natural way. She wasn't mistaking my sex; we were standing in a women's restroom. She looked at me again, gave me a small, understanding smile, and her gaze deepened.

"A nice boy" in a twenty-seven year-old female body.

Not a wanna-be man. Not a damaged soul in gender crisis.

A nice boy.

My face felt hot with the realization that this stranger, this odd girl, saw me for who I actually was.

Then a gruff man's voice called out, "You still in there, Princess? Truck's about to roll, with or without you."

The girl hitched her bag on her shoulder.

"Are you running from someone?" I asked. "The guy on the phone?"

"I told you. Forget it."

She walked out of the bathroom, and I followed behind her.

Two young guys in paint-splattered T-shirts and pants stood by the coolers that held the beer, talking and laughing. A heavyset older guy at the counter held a Playboy and a bag of beef jerky. He met the girl's eyes, and said, "Thought I'd lost ya, Sweetheart."

She went out the front door and didn't speak to him. I picked up my pace to follow her.

Grey Trousers yelled, "Hey! Usin' our facilities means ya buy something, girl."

I grabbed a Milky Way off the shelf, waved it at the woman behind the register, pulled my wallet out of my back pocket.

The woman moved like a tortoise, and the cash register was an antique. I tapped my toe as the heavy guy with the Playboy followed the girl outside. I watched through the front window as he slid his arm across her shoulders and she pushed him away.

I left without getting my change.

"You said a short detour off the Interstate," the girl said. "Now I have no idea where I am."

The man shrugged, then said, "Suit yourself," and walked off.

The girl peeled off her green leather jacket, and sighed. Underneath she wore a white T-shirt tucked into tight blue jeans. She fumbled with her backpack, pulled out a pack of cigarettes and a lighter.

"I can give you a ride," I said. "I'll take you where you need to go."

The two painter guys came out of the store. She looked at them, then back at me.

"You care if I smoke?"

I shook my head.

She hesitated, looked up and down the two-lane road, at the long stretch of nothing in either direction. Then she opened the passenger door of my car and jammed her things into the small space behind the seat.

"My name's Cay," she said. "With a C."

"Like an island."

"Yeah, a small sandy island. That's me."

She stood straight up, stretched her spine, extended her arms to the sky, as if she needed the preparation before confining herself to my car. She was even taller than I'd realized. Her movements were deliberate and fluid, with an occasional nervous twitch.

"My name's Robin," I said. "But no one calls me that."

She tapped a cigarette out of her pack, propped her ass casually against my fender. Her stare was large and questioning.

"Dean," I said. "Most people call me Dean."

"Much better. I agree."

I shifted, pulled my baseball cap off and ran my fingers through my stubbly hair.

"You had a pro do that, didn't you?"

"Yeah," I said. "My friend Theo owns a salon."

She twitched her head back and forth.

"Did mine myself. Get what ya pay for, they say." She grinned, as if she were telling me a devilish secret.

I rearranged things in the car, and she folded herself into the passenger's seat, propped her knees against the dash.

We were only a few minutes from the border, where the dense green thicket of Tennessee became industrial Alabama. Factory smoke and smog.

She didn't talk much. She kept squeezing her battered cell phone. Opening it, then closing it. She knocked it against the window frame a few times. She was having a war with the thing. I almost told her to go ahead and use it, call whoever it was she wanted to yell at. But I wasn't the one stopping her. She looked like she was taking a bullet every time she flipped it open, then shut it again.

I told her I wasn't planning on hitting the big cities, or driving the Interstate. The point of my trip was to take it slow, see some things you couldn't see from the fast lane. But I said I'd take her to the highway or a city, if that's what she wanted.

"Just drive," she said. "Pretend like I'm not here."

That was hard to do. But I listened to my music, tried not to bother her with questions. Though I couldn't stop wondering who she was, where she was from, what kind of demons were racing around inside her skull.

It was still daylight when we rolled into Florence, Alabama, a small city I'd picked out in advance as a place I could stay for the night. I pulled into a Holiday Inn and stopped. I was tired, caked with sweat, ready to stop driving for the day, but I said, "It's about an hour more to the Interstate. You want me to take you?"

She looked toward the hotel.

Then her phone rang. She stared at it a minute, and I wasn't sure she was going to answer. But finally, she flipped it open, and said, "What?"

I got out of the car, thought I'd give her some privacy. But all the windows were down and I could hear everything she said from quite a distance.

"No" was what she said most. Over and over. "No, No, NO—" Her voice growing louder, more insistent. Then finally, "Because I don't want to be found. Because I'm not coming back."

Then she was silent for a long time, the phone still on her ear. She gripped her hair as she listened, then banged her fist to her forehead.

I went into the hotel lobby.

The desk clerk was plump but pretty. I asked if she had two rooms, and she did. I looked out the window. Cay was out of the car, smoking a cigarette. No sign of the cell phone. She caught my eye and came inside.

"No smoking in here," the clerk said, quickly.

Cay stepped back to the door, and flicked the lit cigarette into the parking lot. When she approached again, she shot the clerk a look I hoped I'd never see again. Hatred sharp as a blade.

"Did you decide about the Interstate?" I asked.

"Not tonight," Cay said. "Let's stay here."

Then she stepped in front of me, leaned on the counter, and said to the clerk, "Do you have a king room? I like a big bed."

There was something raw about the way she said it. I felt my legs go stiff.

"Two?" the clerk asked. "You wanted two rooms, right?"

"No," Cay said. "Just one room."

I looked down at my boots, and Cay slid her leg toward me. She reached her hand behind her back and brushed my arm, as if she'd done it a million times before. Her touch was warm and not afraid to reach me, right there in the lobby of a hotel in Florence, Alabama. I inched closer to her, and when I looked up, the clerk was staring at me.

"I do have a king," she said. "Second floor okay?"

"Yeah," I said. "That's great."

The room was generic, mass-produced brown and green décor. Cay went straight to the bathroom and I stood there, between the king-size bed and the mirror, not sure what to do. I'd insisted on paying for the room. Cay didn't argue and I thought maybe she didn't have any money.

I heard the shower kick on.

When she emerged from the bathroom her hair was wet and dark. It made her face seem paler, and more delicate. She wore a large men's T-shirt that hung to her thighs. I tried not to stare at her smooth, bare legs, but she caught me, and smiled. Then she stepped toward the bed.

My duffle bag sat open. She peeked inside, then said, "You have a girlfriend somewhere?"

"Chicago."

"You love her?"

"I don't know."

She sat down on the bed, crossed her legs and raised an eyebrow. She had another tattoo just above her right ankle, a

Chinese character.

"Love," she said.

"What?"

She reached down and stroked the tattoo. "I've never been in love. Not real true love. Maybe it's just a fantasy anyway. But this is mine. You know? It's under my skin. Doesn't matter what else happens."

I nodded, and watched her fingers circle the tattoo, slowly.

"Was that your boyfriend on the phone? Husband?"

She moved her hands away from her ankle. She folded her arms across her chest. "I'm crazy, but not quite crazy enough to marry him."

"Is everything okay? I couldn't help but overhear."

"It's a game we play," she said. "He's an asshole. And I run away. He keeps getting worse. I keep getting farther. One day I'm gonna make it to California. One day I'm gonna save up and buy a goddamned plane ticket. Stop relying on the kindness of strangers to put miles between him and me."

"Is that what I am? A kind stranger?" She stood up, and stepped toward me.

"Yes," she said. "I think you are the very kindest kind of stranger."

"I would have gotten you your own room."

"I know."

"Do you need money? For a bus or a train?"

She took my hand in hers, brought it up to her face.

"A plane ticket to California?"

"You're crazier than me," she said. Then she kissed the tips of each of my fingers, lightly, and ended with her tongue tickling the center of my palm.

I took her face in my hands, and kissed her.

The sex wasn't urgent or fast, the way I usually liked it. I never went to my bag, never pulled out equipment. She wouldn't let me. When I asked, she shook her head, said she wanted to feel *me* inside of her, not something artificial. Then she closed her eyes, put my fingers deep into her wet mouth. I stopped thinking after that. Stopped worrying and wondering if I was enough. Stopped trying to reach for something that wasn't there. I lost track of everything except the feel of Cay's naked body under mine. Nothing between us but skin, and sex flowing natural as rain.

When I woke up, it was still and quiet. I didn't remember falling asleep, didn't hear the door, or her movement away. But it was morning and the sun spilled through a crack in the curtain, and Cay was gone.

We'd made love for hours, until exhaustion had overtaken us both. We'd stayed there, wrapped in each other's arms, content in our shared damp heat. We didn't talk. There didn't seem to be a need for words, nor any urgency.

I waited around awhile, searched the room for a note, or some other sign she might be coming back. But there was nothing. My wallet was in my jeans pocket, and all my money was still there. I felt like a shit as I opened it and wondered. But it was untouched. I would have given her whatever she needed, if she'd asked. Then I remembered her face in the women's restroom in Tennessee. How she didn't want to involve me in her mess. Because I was a nice boy.

I checked out of the hotel just before noon, drove around Florence, looking up and down side streets, peering into store windows. I thought about staying, about waiting at the hotel another night, hoping she'd return. But there was something about the way she'd clutched that cell phone, how she fought and fought with it, that made me know she was really gone. Back to him, most likely. So, I got back on the road and headed south, alone.

Every turn I made led to another town full of factories, the air stale and close. I searched for a park or a forest or a lake.

I found it in Gadsden. Noccalula Falls. A waterfall in central Alabama.

It took a few hours to get there, and as I drove, I imagined

Cay still with me. I imagined her telling me about California. The white sand of the desert, the rocky cliffs of the coastline, months of no rain. I tried not to imagine the boyfriend on the other end of that cell phone. Or the next kind stranger she'd hitch with, on her way back to him.

I tried my best not to think about the ache in my chest I didn't recognize, or understand.

The park was large, but not deserted, even on a Wednesday afternoon. The plateau basin was nearly dry, the falls diluted, not like the pictures in the glossy brochure, which must have been taken right after a heavy downpour. But nearly a hundred feet of falling water is impressive any day. So I took out my camera and shot it from every angle.

When I finally put the camera down, I looked around, not sure what or who I expected to see. But there was nothing. No one waiting. No one looking for me. No one clutching a cell phone, hoping I'd call. There were just the trees, a sweet city park, and the water falling.

I didn't stop again until I crossed the line into Georgia. I bought a bag of peaches on the side of the road and ate them as I drove, juice running down my chin. The red clay on the shoulder made me want to stop and dig my fingers in, but I kept driving. Just before the Florida border, I looked at the gas gauge and pulled into the next station, below empty. I restocked my cooler with water and Coke and asked the clerk if there was a decent restaurant or hotel within fifty miles.

"Tallahassee's your best bet," he said. "Thirty minutes east."

I went there, got a room at a Quality Inn. I changed into khakis and a collar shirt, found a steak joint where I had a beer and a New York strip. When I finished, I was full, tired, but keyed up.

Across the room was a short, stocky waitress with sideburns and a scowl. I nodded at her as I paid my check, but she ignored me.

I walked over, looked her straight in the eye, and said, "Can you help me out? I'm not from here. Is there a bar? Someplace friendly?"

"One," she said. "Guys mostly. Nothing worth seeing during the week."

"That's cool."

She gave me directions, then walked away without further conversation.

I didn't want to dance, and I didn't want to pick anyone up. But I couldn't go back to the room so soon. I could still feel Cay's body resting against mine. I could still smell her under my skin.

So I went to the bar. Three old queens playing pool and a juke box with nothing but Patsy Cline and disco. I ordered a beer, spun around on the stool, propped myself on my elbows, and watched the place like the nature channel.

I ran my hand from my scalp, down my body, letting it fall between my knees.

The front door opened and a guy about forty walked in, black leather jacket over a hairy chest. In Chicago I would have thought him pathetic. In Tallahassee, he was real.

He walked up and ordered a whiskey. Then looked at me, surprised.

"It's a guy place, I know."

"Just won't get any play in here, that's all," he said.

"Not looking for it tonight."

He turned out to be a good listener. His eyes were soft and kind, and I surprised myself at how much I said. Somewhere in Georgia I'd realized how much I'd wanted to tell Cay, how much I'd wanted to ask her, to get to know her. But I was in shock at how well she seemed to know me, without effort, and without confusion. Then she'd left me in Alabama without a word and I was sure I'd never see her again. So, I told this random guy in the only gay bar in Tallahassee everything there was to know about my screwed-up life. Gender and sex and love and all I feared wasn't possible for someone like me.

After our beers had been empty awhile and the bartender had begun to ignore us, he leaned in close, tugged on my sleeve, and said, "Just because you screw like a guy doesn't make you one. It's just sex, right?"

"It wasn't just sex last night," I said. "Not for me. It felt like the start of something. Something different."

His eyes were shifty and he swayed on his stool. He was drunk and I'd never felt more sober.

"You're a pretty boy," he said. "Maybe you're the kind of boy I'd like to take home after all."

I smiled, uneasy.

He was so close I could smell his sweat, his whiskey breath.

I stood up, shook his hand, and said, "It was real nice talking with you."

He leaned back, laughed, and winked at me. "See. Now you know one kind of man you're not."

I was in bed, alone, asleep, before midnight.

In the morning, I decided not to stop again, except for gas, until I got to Miami. I stayed on the back roads, twisting through old Florida towns, main streets lined with moss-covered shady oaks. I drove twelve hours until I was on South Beach, sand between my toes. It was already dark and I didn't have a reservation at a resort, didn't have friends or family to visit. I changed clothes in a public restroom on the beach, washed my face in the dirty sink. I'd picked my final destination for its club scene. The long, wild strip full of neon lights and techno vibrations. But now that I was there, I had no interest. I lay down on the sandy beach, and used my duffle as a pillow.

I'd hoped my long journey south would clear my head. Hoped I'd make some decisions, about myself, my relationship with Barb, my life. But I couldn't think about any of that. Because when I looked out at the unlit Atlantic, the vast darkness beyond, all I could see was the face of a girl who said, "You're a nice boy."

The kindest kind.

So I closed my eyes, and remembered kissing her. Touching her with only my skin, my fingers, my mouth.

"You don't need anything else," she'd told me.

Without explanation, I believed her. The girl with love under her skin. Who I hoped would someday make it all the way to California. Where she would sit alone, too, on a soft sandy beach, and hear the waves crashing in. And maybe then, at the end of her long journey west, she'd remember a boy she met in Tennessee. Not a random guy she shared a room with for the night. But a nice boy she loved once in Florence, Alabama. That's what I was praying for, when I pushed myself deeper into the sand, wrapped my arms around my chest, and waited for the sun to rise.

DEBORAH ALLBRITAIN resides in San Diego, CA. She received the Patricia Dobler Poetry Prize in 2017 and has received nominations for the Pushcart Prize and the Best of the Net. Deborah's book manuscripts have been semi-finalists and individual poems have been finalists in the *Crab Creek Review* Poetry Contest, the Wabash Poetry Prize, the Bellingham Prize for Poetry, the *Florida Review* Editors' Award, and the *Comstock Review* Poetry Contest. Her poems have appeared in *The Beloit Poetry Journal*, *BODY Literature*, *Greensboro Review*, *The Laurel Review*, *The MacGuffin*, *Salamander*, and *Sugar House Review*. Deborah has work forthcoming in *Ecotone*.

BENJAMIN BALTHASER is the author of *Dedication*, a collection of poems about Jewish victims of second red scare, and *Anti-Imperialist Modernism*, on transnational social movements and making of modernism in the U.S. His work has been published in journals such as *American Quarterly*, *Boston Review*, *Minnesota Review*, and elsewhere. He lives in Chicago.

RITA WELTY BOURKE is the author of *Islomanes of Cumberland Island* and *Kylie's Ark: The Making of a Veterinarian*. She has published fiction and nonfiction in numerous literary journals.

PATRICIA BUDD has been published in *The MacGuffin*, *Naugatuck River Review*, *The Maine Review*, *Night & Sparrow*, *Anderbo*, and several other journals and anthologies. She studied engineering math and literature at Sarah Lawrence College, took her M.F.A. at Stonecoast in 2006, and intermittently teaches poetry and writing at her local Osher Lifelong Learning Institute (OLLI). She was the editor of *Reflections*, OLLI's literary magazine, for several years. A Reiki Master and certified nutrition coach, Patricia enjoys hiking on the coast of Maine.

BILL CHRISTOPHERSEN'S fifth poetry collection, *Why the Gods Don't Get It*, will be published shortly by Kelsay Books. Several recent poems of his will be featured in the journal *Hanging Loose*, issue number 113.

MARYANN CORBETT is the author of five books of poetry, most recently *In Code* from Able Muse Press. Her work has won the Richard Wilbur Book Award and the Willis Barnstone Translation Prize and has been published in venues like *Southwest Review, Barrow Street, Rattle, River Styx, Atlanta Review, The Evansville Review, Measure, Literary Imagination, The Dark Horse*, and *Subtropics*. Her poems have been featured on *Poetry Daily, Verse Daily, American Life in Poetry, The Poetry Foundation*, and *The Writer's Almanac*, and in an assortment of anthologies including *The Best American Poetry 2018*.

ED FALCO is the author of a dozen books, including novels, short story collections, and poetry collections. His most recent book is the poetry collection *Wolf Moon Blood Moon* (LSU, 2018). His novel, *Transcendent Gardening*, is forthcoming from C&R Press in 2022. A recipient of the Robert Penn Warren Prize in Poetry from *The Southern Review*, and the Emily Clark Balch Prize in Fiction from *Virginia Quarterly Review*, he teaches in the MFA Program in Creative Writing at Virginia Tech.

GARY FINCKE'S books have won the Flannery O'Connor Prize for Short Fiction, The Robert C. Jones Prize for Short Nonfiction Prose, and the Wheeler Prize for Poetry. His latest poetry collections are *The Infinity Room* (2019), which won Michigan State's Wheelbarrow Press Prize, and *The Mussolini Diaries* (2020, Serving House).

AMANDA GAINES is an Appalachian writer and Ph.D. candidate in CNF in OSU's creative writing program. Her poetry and nonfiction are published or awaiting publication in *Typehouse*, *Pithead Chapel*, *Yemassee*, *Redivider*, *New Orleans Review*, *Southeast Review*, *The Southern Review*, *Juked*, *Rattle*, *New South*, *SmokeLong Quarterly*, *Ninth Letter*, and *Superstition Review*.

JASON GEBHARDT'S poems have appeared in a number of journals, including *The Southern Review*, *Poet Lore*, *Tinderbox Poetry Journal*, *Iron Horse Literary Review*, and *Crab Creek Review*. His chapbook *Good Housekeeping* was a semifinalist in the 2016 Frost Place Chapbook Competition and won *Main Street Rag*'s 2016 Cathy Smith Bowers Prize. He is the recipient of multiple Artist Fellowships awarded by the DC Commission on the Arts and Humanities.

MAEGAN GONZALES is a multi-disciplinary artist and the daughter of a magician. Much of her time before her own children was borrowed and spent bartering black hats and white rabbits. Currently she lives in southwest Louisiana with her family where she teaches English, propagates plants, and spills entirely too much coffee. Her poetry has appeared or is forthcoming in *New Orleans Review*, *The Hunger*, *High Shelf Press*, *Big Muddy*, *Elephant Journal*, and others. She holds an M.A. and M.F.A. from McNeese State University. Connect and follow her musings on Instagram @maery_gonzales.

BANZELMAN GURET is from Connecticut. His most recent work has appeared in *New Orleans Review*.

Originally born and raised in upstate New York, **CHRISTOPHER HEFFERNAN** has had poetry and fiction placed in magazines and journals around the country such as *The Believer, The Writer's Journal, Pacific Coast Journal, Cottonwood, Talking River, The South Dakota Review, Louisiana Literature, The Sierra Nevada Review, The Tampa Review, Whiskey Island, Big Muddy,* and *The Madison Review.* He has a book of poetry and flash fiction titled *Rag Water,* and spends much of his time working and walking in the sun.

CHRISTIAN HOLT is a graduate of the University of Wisconsin's M.F.A. program in fiction. His work has appeared or is upcoming in *Gargoyle, The Southeast Review, Front Porch Journal, F(r)iction,* and *The Woven Tale Press,* among others. He lives in San Francisco with his pet Roomba, Isildur.

HYAN HYUN-OCK IM was born in Seoul, and now lives in New York City, where she is a proofreader in the advertising industry. She has a B.F.A. in painting and an M.A. in TESOL. She has an extensive background in the Korean film industry. Her nonfiction and fiction have appeared in *Knot, Chew, Moonrabbit Review,* and *The Greensboro Review.* She is now writing a novel set in South Korea in the early 1980s.

LEN KRUGER'S fiction has appeared in *Zoetrope: All-Story, The Barcelona Review, Gargoyle, District Fray,* and the anthology *This Is What America Looks Like: Fiction and Poetry from DC, Maryland, and Virginia.* He lives in Washington, D.C. More online at lenkruger.com.

EDDIE KRZEMINSKI received his M.F.A. from Florida International University. His work has appeared or is forthcoming in *Grist, Split Lip, Sinking City,* and elsewhere. He teaches writing classes in Southwest Florida.

Rooja Mohassessy is an Iranian-born poet and educator living in Northern California. Her poems have appeared or are forthcoming in *Narrative Magazine, Poet Lore, RHINO Poetry, California Fire and Water: An Anthology of Poems, Southern Humanities Review, CALYX Journal, Ninth Letter, Bare Life Review, The Florida Review, New Letters*, and elsewhere. Rooja is a 2021 recipient of the MacDowell Fellowship and a student at the M.F.A. program at Pacific University, Oregon. She reads for *Prairie Schooner*.

Mary Lynn Reed's fiction has appeared, or will soon appear, in *Mississippi Review, Colorado Review, Free State Review, Reunion: The Dallas Review*, and many other places. She has an M.F.A. in Creative Writing from University of Maryland. She lives in western New York with her wife, and together they co-edit the online literary journal *MoonPark Review*.

Jennifer Savran Kelly's (she/her/they/them) debut novel *Endpapers* is forthcoming from Algonquin Books. Her short fiction has appeared in *Black Warrior Review, Hobart, Green Mountains Review* (online), *Iron Horse Literary Review*, and elsewhere. Jennifer lives in Ithaca, New York, where she writes, binds books, and works as a production editor at Cornell University Press.

Peter Serchuk's poems have appeared in a variety of journals, including *New Letters, Boulevard, Denver Quarterly, Atlanta Review, Valparaiso Poetry Review*, and other places. His latest book is *The Purpose of Things* (Regal House), a collection of short poems and photographs created in collaboration with photographer Pieter de Koninck. More at peterserchuk.com.

Naomi Thiers grew up in California and Pittsburgh, but her chosen home is Washington DC/Northern Virginia. She is author of four poetry collections: *Only the Raw Hands Are Heaven* (WWPH), *In Yolo County*, and *She Was a Cathedral* (Finishing Line Press) and *Made of Air* (Kelsay Books). Her poems, book reviews, and essays have been published in *Virginia Quarterly Review*, *Poet Lore*, *Colorado Review*, *Grist*, *Sojourners*, and many other magazines and anthologies. Former editor of the journal *Phoebe*, she works as a magazine editor and lives on the banks of Four Mile Run in Arlington, Virginia.

CHRIS VANJONACK is an M.F.A. candidate at the University of Illinois at Urbana-Champaign, a reader at *Ninth Letter*, and a former language arts teacher from Fort Collins, Colorado. He is a recipient of the 2020 AWP Intro Journals Award, and his fiction and creative non-fiction have appeared or are forthcoming in *One Story*, *Barrelhouse*, *Diagram*, *The Rumpus*, *CRAFT Literary*, and elsewhere. Find him on Twitter @chrisvanjonack and read more stories at chrisvanjonack.com.

FRANCINE WITTE'S poetry and fiction have appeared in *Smokelong Quarterly*, *Wigleaf*, *Mid-American Review*, and *Passages North*. Her latest books are *Dressed All Wrong for This* (Blue Light Press,) *The Way of the Wind* (AdHoc fiction,) and *The Theory of Flesh* (Kelsay Books.) Her chapbook, *The Cake, The Smoke, The Moon* (flash fiction) was published by ELJ September, 2021. She is flash fiction editor for *Flash Boulevard* and *The South Florida Poetry Journal*. She lives in NYC.

www.ingramcontent.com/pod-product-compliance
Lightning Source LLC
Chambersburg PA
CBHW020752210626
46807CB00018B/2690